THE ENIGMAS OF HUGO LACKLAN

In *The Enigmas of Hugo Lacklan*, Alexander Dunkley relates some of the puzzling anecdotes of his social anthropologist friend. Though quite unacademic, these questions, and others, intrigue Hugo. In *The Vanishing Punk*, how did the punk thief vanish after his crimes? And we can only wonder what the reason was for the odd behaviour of *The Five Elderly Gentlemen*. Then, in *The Expensive Daub*, why were hideous daubs selling for such high prices from a London gallery?

JOHN LIGHT

THE
ENIGMAS OF
HUGO LACKLAN

Complete and Unabridged

LINFORD
Leicester

First published in Great Britain

First Linford Edition
published 2012

This is a work of fiction. No connection is intended with any real person, alive or dead. The events chronicled here have not yet happened (as far as I know).

British Library CIP Data

Light, John, *1943* –
   The enigmas of Hugo Lacklan. - -
(Linford mystery library)
1. Detective and mystery stories, English.
2. Large type books.
I. Title II. Series
823.9'14–dc23

ISBN 978–1–4448–1365–4

Published by
F. A. Thorpe (Publishing)
Anstey, Leicestershire

Set by Words & Graphics Ltd.
Anstey, Leicestershire
Printed and bound in Great Britain by
T. J. International Ltd., Padstow, Cornwall

This book is printed on acid-free paper

5 01465051

Versions of some of these stories have appeared before:

'Allergy'
in *Fisheye* (1986) and *Premonitions* (1993)

'A Nineteenth Century Dream'
in *Beyond the Boundaries* (1996)

'Artisitic Licence'
in *Dial 174* (1994)

'Bequest'
in *Melodic Scribble* (1985) and
The White Rose (1990)

'Opus Posthumous'
in *Black Rose* (2000)

'Proof'
in *Auguries* (1988) and *Gentle Reader* (1997)

'The Expensive Daub'
in *Saccade* (1999)

'The Five Elderly Gentlemen'
in *Paladin* (1993)

'The Man Who Wrote Letters'
in *Shadows* (2005)

'The Sound of the Sea'
in *Dream Science Fiction* (1989)

The Five Elderly Gentlemen

Hugo Lacklan and I were strolling along the glen in the direction of the mediaeval castle where he has his rooms. His College pays only a peppercorn rent for the ancient pile built, I believe, by an ancestor of Harry Hotspur. Even so, it is a drain on the institution's resources, merely to maintain and heat it. The expense, however, is borne for the sake of the prestige and presence which the grandeur of the battlemented fortress bestows on the whole University. Hugo, of course, enjoys this setting, as though the castle were his own, and he the lord of its extensive parkland.

The ground sloped away from us towards the distant towers and the wide metalled track made for easy walking, so that we were able to converse comfortably.

Perhaps I should introduce myself. My name is Alexander Dunkley. Although there are times when I am tempted to deny it, Hugo Lacklan is my friend and on occasion, although I am loath to admit it, I find myself admiring his insights, while deploring his outrageously high opinion of himself. Thus I feel a strange compulsion to describe some of the enigmas in which he has involved me in the hope that they may interest others. Hugo and I have known each other for decades and several of these events took place a good while ago. Such is the acceleration of change that the world in which they happened already seems unfamiliar.

Unfortunately I have no real talent as a raconteur. I am a scientist and my style of writing has been shaped more by the exigencies of scientific reportage than the opportunities of literature. Nevertheless I have done my best and if you find my prose dull or awkward I can only apologise and hope it will not detract too seriously from the singular nature of the events themselves.

To continue then, I was teasing Hugo about his seigniorial delusions, but he merely smiled.

'It's true I enjoy living in the castle,' he rejoined, 'but I would not remain if the duties my residence entails were not also enjoyable.'

'Then you are an even more unusual person than I had supposed,' I mocked. 'I suspect many people would — in fact, do — accept obligations and restraints which they find downright detestable in order to live in the surroundings and style they imagine they enjoy. Think of the city commuter who daily endures hell to earn an inflated salary in the metropolis, while owning a house in a distant suburb.'

'Doubtless you are right,' he conceded. 'Indeed, I once came across a very interesting example of just such an attitude.'

I knew at once that a story was coming. I could tell by the tone of his voice, the slightly abstracted expression on his face, and the way his gait had slowed.

'No!' I said firmly. 'I will not listen to yet another of your dolorous tales prophesying doom and gloom for Mankind — or, at any rate, for vast sections of it. Save them for your students! They're made of sterner stuff than I!'

It wasn't that I believed any of Hugo's bizarre anecdotes, but, well, they did leave a nasty insidious doubt, like the aftertaste of a particularly vile homemade wine. I was thinking especially of the enigma of his Uncle Joseph's diary, and the horrifying history of Magnus Thoren.

'There's nothing to worry you in the little incident I propose to relate,' protested Hugo. 'It has no dire consequence for the rest of the world; indeed, it never had any consequence for anyone but the five elderly gentlemen themselves.'

I struggled, but knew I was hooked. How was it that he always managed to herald these stories by some intriguing phrase? In this case, it was the five elderly gentlemen. What on earth could have interested Hugo in elderly gentlemen, and why five? What was it that separated that handful of old men from all other old men in the world?

We had come to a collection of stone slabs which had been assembled into a rude but not uninviting seat, with a fine view across the gorse-covered slopes to a sombre wood, and beyond to the rosy sandstone of the obsolescent fastness that commanded the strategic route to the South through this once turbulent land. We settled ourselves on the rough bench.

'It began with a letter from my Aunt Emily, who lives in Barrow-in-Furness. She's a great-aunt, really, but I always called her Aunt Em as a boy, and the inaccuracy seems trivial.'

It was typical of Hugo to have a great-aunt in Barrow, just as he has an uncle in Haltwhistle, a cousin in Marsh Gibbon and friends in all sorts of oddly named places.

'I don't often see her now, but we exchange cards and I always send her copies of my scientific papers — not because I think she might read them but because I know that she feels some quite unjustifiable pride in collecting them. Mind you, the letter I received did make me wonder if she had, at any rate, read

5

some of the abstracts.

'The letter was quite short. I can probably quote it almost word for word.'

This was another of Hugo's irritating accomplishments. He had an almost photographic memory, which was the bane of his students' lives. He closed his eyes.

'*Dear Hugo,* (Aunt Emily wrote) *Thank you for your most recent paper which I'm sure was ever so clever. I don't know where you get your brains from. You certainly don't take after your mother, and I never did like your father. Perhaps you're a throwback to my own parents' generation. Anyway, it prompted me to write to you about a little mystery that's been intriguing me. I thought it might be just the thing for one of your articles on the strange things people do.*'

(I couldn't help smiling at Great-Aunt Emily's description of what a social anthropologist does. I decided I might quite like Aunt Em.)

'*I think I've told you before that I usually go to Pickering and Fosgill's for my lunch. I don't like those modern*

6

places in Dalton Road. The gangways really are too narrow for me and there are always pools of cold coffee on the tables. Of course, I used to go to the Co-op, but I can't manage the stairs anymore, and Pickering and Fosgill's have a lift up to the restaurant.'

'Do you really expect me to believe you can recall word for word such a rambling letter?' I interrupted.

'Why not?' asked Hugo ambiguously. 'Of course, if I'm boring you, I'll say not another word.'

'No, really, it isn't that; it's just that your aunt's prose, charming in its way of course, doesn't seem entirely to the point.'

'On the contrary; it is very much so. Almost every word I've repeated to you proved of great significance. She went on to say that her favourite table was close to the window, where she could look down into the street if there was nothing of interest to observe in the restaurant. *There is a most obliging girl there*, she wrote, *who always keeps the table free for me, if she can, which is almost every day,*

7

since *Pickering and Fosgill's is not as popular as it used to be when I was young. Sometimes indeed, I and the four elderly gentlemen are the only customers.'*

'Four?' I interrupted again. 'I thought you said five before.' I daresay I was a little sharp, thinking to have caught Hugo in an inconsistency at last.

'Certainly I did,' he admonished, 'and five elderly gentlemen there were, as you'll shortly hear, if you'll only refrain from butting-in. As I was saying, Aunt Emily was often alone in the restaurant, apart from the four elderly gentlemen, and of course the waitress. So she naturally took particular note of the men. Again, I quote her own words.

'*Although I say four, there are actually five men, but only four are ever there together. On Mondays, there is the bald man with the rheumy eyes who wears the blue pin-stripe; the rather distinguished grey-haired gentleman with the neat moustache and the silk handkerchief in the breast pocket of his tweed jacket; and the shaky, stoop-shouldered old man,*

8

with the disagreeable sniff. Finally, there is the one who likes to think he's really much younger than the others and leers at the waitress in a quite disgraceful way. He wears a blazer with a large badge on the pocket, and a tie with little badges all over it.

'On Tuesdays, the bald man's place is taken by a tall thin gentleman in a blue serge suit. He has a mournful expression and hardly speaks. Then, on Wednesdays, the bald man is back in his place and the amorous gentleman is absent.

'So it continues through Thursday and Friday, until by the end of the week, each one of them has been absent on just one day. Each of them has their own set day of the week, and it never varies. This has been going on ever since I started to lunch at Pickering and Fosgill's, and I would dearly love to know what's behind it all. I dare say there's some simple explanation, but it baffles me. It certainly isn't anything to do with the accommodation in the restaurant. There are several tables which would sit five or even six, and which are scarcely ever occupied.

Well, Hugo, do you think their behaviour is curious enough to study? I do hope you'll think so, and that you'll come and investigate.'

Hugo paused.

'The rest of the letter was taken up with news of cousins and other relatives, and I won't bore you with it.' He half turned to look at me, and he raised his eyebrows quizzically.

'What do you make of it?' he asked.

'Nothing, really,' I answered. 'It certainly is an odd circumstance. There must be an explanation, but I confess I can't see it.'

'You can't? You disappoint me. I could immediately see a number of theories which would fit the facts, although it turned out that none of my initial ideas were right.'

He brooded on the unaccountability of this for a few moments, while I watched trees moving in the breeze back up the glen, before returning my gaze to the prospect of the castle with its four battlemented towers, in one of which Hugo has his rooms.

'Of course, I went. I'm fond of Aunt Emily and I like Barrow, and I decided a trip to Furness would make a welcome change. I drove over, along the military road to Carlisle, down through the Lakes on the M6, and across the Furness peninsula through Ulverston and Dalton. My aunt has a house in a quiet, well-to-do part of the town. It's too big for her, really, but it belonged to her parents and she'd never dream of moving.

'I arrived on a Saturday, expecting to clear up my Great-Aunt's mystery over the weekend and then spend some time walking the lonelier western fells. Although it was past lunch time, I suggested we go to Pickering and Fosgill's for tea and to spy out the land. My aunt was surprised. 'Pickering and Fosgill have never opened on Saturdays or Sundays,' she said.

'Of course, I should have realised that from her letter. Had the restaurant been open at the weekend, it would have upset the pattern.'

(The trouble with writing this kind of prose, reporting what someone else tells one is it becomes recursive and I get confused by all those embedded speech marks, so I'm going to relate this as though I was Hugo — I'm fairly sure I can tell it as he did.)

'You may take me to the Old Mill, if you wish,' said Aunt Em. 'They do a nice afternoon tea there.' So I drove her out along the coast road and we joined the throng of devotees of afternoon tea. Most of them were elderly, but there were a few families; the parents anxiously supervising their offspring, for the Old Mill is no formica-tabled snack bar.

On Monday, we went for lunch at Pickering and Fosgill's. The food was solid but at least it was hot. We sat in a fuscous atmosphere of antique comfort on polished wooden chairs at a table set with a white cloth. The walls were covered in gloomy damask and there was a deep maroon carpet on the floor which added to the gloom.

'Here they come,' whispered my aunt.

I heard a number of people ascending the stairs. They were exactly as Great-Aunt Emily had described them and I had a distinct feeling of déja-vu. I applied myself to the brown Windsor soup, while studying the four newcomers covertly. They had taken a table at the opposite side of the room and spoke in the lowered tones appropriate to the sepulchral air of the place, so that there was no prospect of eavesdropping. I knew better than to suggest to my aunt that we move to a table closer to them!

I had already worked out in advance my plan of campaign. It seemed clear to me that there could be no reason connected with the restaurant itself for the peculiar rota operated by the five elderly gentlemen. I must confess that in this I was quite wrong; even so, my actions were sound — despite being predicated on false reasoning.

Aunt Em and I took our time over the roast beef and Yorkshire pudding, the ice cream and tinned peaches, and then sipped our coffee slowly. At last, the four elderly gentlemen dabbed at their lips with their paper napkins and rose to leave.

'They must have an account here,' whispered my aunt, 'as they never pay at the kiosk.'

I leaned across the table.

'I'll meet you in the library,' I murmured. So saying, I abandoned my ancient relative and set off in pursuit of the four elderly gentlemen.

At the bottom of the tiled staircase, they bade each other a perfunctory farewell beneath the Victorian stained glass window and then separated. I did not hesitate, having already marked my quarry as the bald man who, if events followed their previous pattern, would not be present for lunch in Pickering and Fosgill's on the following day.

My target, as they say in films, walked to the corner of the street and turned into a narrow lane which eventually opened into the road leading to the bus station. There he caught a local service and I did likewise.

The bus took us out across the dockyard to Vickers Town on Walney Island. The bald man alighted at the terminus and I followed him into an ugly modern housing estate. We hadn't gone far when he stopped outside some old people's bungalows. Taking a key from his pocket, he stepped up to a front door and went in. I looked about. The street was deserted and there was no corner shop. It didn't look as though I would discover anything about the man by prowling around, so I got the next bus back into Barrow itself and walked along to the public library, where I found my aunt sitting patiently at a table with a pile of books in front of her.

'Find any you haven't already read?' I teased her.

'They always save the new books for me as they come in,' she answered. 'It's very kind of them. However, I'm more interested in our real life mystery. What did you discover?'

She was a little disappointed at my efforts when I told her.

'Why didn't you knock at the door and pretend to be a Jehovah's Witness, or something?' she reproved. 'You might have found out a bit more.' I smiled.

'I may not be able to join you for lunch tomorrow,' I parried. 'It seems clear that the key to the mystery lies in what each of them does when they're not at lunch with

15

the others. I intend to observe the bald-headed man tomorrow.'

My aunt brightened up.

'Do you think they're a gang of some kind?' she asked. 'Each of them doing a desperate crime in turn, while the others have lunch and prepare to swear an alibi if necessary?'

'I hardly think so,' I replied. 'It would be a very amateurish attempt if they did. No, it must be more subtle than that.'

We returned to my car and drove home along Abbey Road.

The next day, I drove out to Walney, and parked on the sea front. I approached the old people's homes on foot. I'd provided myself with a pile of leaflets from a local building society and strolled along the street, pushing one in to each door, glancing at regular intervals towards the bungalows. Although I worked as slowly as I reasonably could, it didn't take me long to complete the deliveries, and there was no sign of the bald-headed man. I'd quite expected that he would be out early, but it seems I was wrong — unless he had gone before I arrived.

I retreated round the corner, took a cap out of my pocket and put on a pair of glasses. I returned to the street and began sketching in an ostentatious manner. If anyone asked me, I would say I was making a series of drawings of local views for the Council's publicity department. A less likely subject for advertising the borough it would have been difficult to find, but people are used to their local council doing idiotic things.

I had begun to think either that he had indeed left before I arrived, or else that he was not going anywhere, when of a sudden the bald-headed man emerged. I put away my sketch pad, and followed him to the terminus, where we caught a bus back into town. Imagine my surprise when the subject of my interest retraced his steps of yesterday. Could he be breaking the pattern which my aunt swore had persisted for months? I glanced at my watch. It was still rather early for lunch. I almost sighed with relief when he walked by the entrance to the restaurant, but was quite startled when he turned the corner and entered the store by a side entrance.

('Well?' At this point in his narrative Hugo looked at me. 'Have you guessed the solution yet?'

I shook my head.

'I fear it is quite straightforward and trivial — I'm almost reluctant to reveal it; it's sure to disappoint you.'

'You certainly aren't going to leave the story there,' I answered hotly. 'I should never listen to another of your ridiculous tales again if you did.'

He smiled, and continued.)

★ ★ ★

As soon as I saw the bald-headed man go in by the side-entrance I tumbled to it, of course. It merely remained for me to prove it to my own satisfaction.

I returned to the front street and before long saw my aunt approaching from the direction of the bus station. I must confess I was touched by how pleased she was to see me, and affected by the sudden realisation of the loneliness of the life she led.

We went up to lunch and all was exactly as normal on a Tuesday, according to Aunt Em. Towards the end of the meal, the waitress brought our coffee as usual, and I made sure she saw the over-generous tip I was leaving by the sugar bowl. As she set our cups down, I looked directly at her.

'I imagine you find Wednesdays rather trying, don't you?' I asked.

She looked at me, startled.

'Or does he behave himself when he's at the sink?'

She grinned then, and answered in a low voice.

'The cook keeps a sharp eye on him, sir. She would never stand for any nonsense in the kitchen, though how you know about it, I can't imagine. I do hope you won't let on what I said. The gentlemen were very insistent it should be a secret.'

As soon as she'd gone, Great-Aunt Emily naturally demanded an explanation, and was amused enough to chuckle out loud when I revealed to her the secret of the five elderly gentlemen.

* ★ ★

Hugo regarded me quizzically.

'I do rather regret having related this anecdote now,' he remarked. 'It really is somewhat banal, and I can't imagine you being as amused as Aunt Em.'

'Oh, get on with it!' I exclaimed impatiently.

'Well, you see, these five elderly gentlemen liked the luxury of dining at Pickering and Fosgill's — a very modest luxury, but even so, one they couldn't really afford. So they came to an arrangement with the management. One of them would do the washing up each day, while the others dined, in lieu of wages!'

The Vanishing Punk

Amusing though some of Hugo Lacklan's stories were, I had never regarded them as other than fantasies. Certainly, I preferred not to do so, since on occasion they would have been distinctly disquieting if taken seriously. So I was determined to be sceptical about his advice to Sebastian Sinclair.

Hugo and I happened to be invited speakers at a three-day Home Office Seminar on developments in forensic science. Since Hugo is a social anthropologist, and I am a chemist, we rarely meet at conferences and only some gathering of an interdisciplinary nature would bring us together professionally. I had been asked to give a short paper on the use of time-of-flight mass spectrometry allied to high pressure liquid chromatography in the detection of sub-microgram quantities of toxic drugs in human serum. Hugo was due to give a lecture on the supposed absence of property-related crimes in certain primitive cultures.

The conference was at the Heriot-Watt University and on the first evening Hugo and I met, almost inevitably, in the bar. As we exchanged pleasantries, Hugo was hailed by a man somewhat our junior, whom he introduced to me as Sebastian Sinclair — Inspector Sinclair, CID, no less! Hugo had been his tutor at the northern university where he is a Professor. As it was an expenses-paid affair, we quickly decided to drink gin and tonic, and repaired to a comfortable alcove with a tray full of bottles, anticipating a convivial evening.

Although Sebastian Sinclair had secured his degree in anthropology, he had entered The Metropolitan Police Force immediately and had made no further use of his specialised knowledge, so he and Hugo had no more to say to each other about their speciality than did Hugo and I about our respective sciences, and the topic of mutual acquaintances was soon exhausted.

I'm not sure exactly how it came about,

but Sinclair was chafing Hugo about the tall stories he used to tell his students — and still does — and Hugo was parrying these jibes with his usual good-natured but unrepentant banter.

'Did he ever tell you about the mystery of the five elderly gentlemen?' I asked Sinclair, and on the latter professing ignorance of it, I prevailed on Hugo to relate it. I did so partly because I thought it would interest Sinclair, being akin to his own line of country, but mostly, I confess, in the hope of catching Hugo out in some inconsistency which would reveal the tale as the pure fabrication I suspected it to be. Sinclair laughed uproariously at the denouement, but I felt a secret satisfaction that he refused to take Hugo's supposed deductive prowess seriously.

'That sort of thing might have been all very well in the days of Sherlock Holmes,' he remarked, 'although personally I think that even then the so-called gifted amateur would have been no match for the professional force. Certainly today there is no place for the likes of Holmes; steady, methodical teamwork is what gets results.'

'You disappoint me,' rejoined Hugo. 'You make modern detection sound very dull. Do you really claim that you have never yourself come across a problem such as might have intrigued Conan Doyle's great protagonist?'

Perhaps it was the alcohol which caused the Inspector to take this enquiry seriously. He reflected for long moments, before confiding seemingly with reluctance.

'Well, as it happens, there is at present a case which presents some features that Holmes might indeed have revelled in and I daresay he could have produced an ingenious explanation of the facts, but I'm certain that the real answer will be much more prosaic than Conan Doyle would ever have allowed.'

'You mean this case is as yet unsolved?' I interposed.

Sinclair nodded with that gravity which only inebriation can produce.

'Then let us put Hugo to the test,' I cried maliciously. 'Lay the facts before him, and let us see what he makes of them.'

I and the gin together were persuasive

and Sinclair soon related all he knew.

'We have been plagued by a series of minor thefts — minor, that is, in these days of multi-million pound heists, although for the victims they are serious enough. All have occurred in shops or other small businesses in the many narrow thoroughfares which open off Oxford Street in the heart of London's West End. There's no doubt that they are all the work of the same man. We have a meticulous description of him. Yet so far he has eluded us.'

'How many robberies has he perpetrated?' I enquired.

'Seventeen,' admitted the Inspector.

'And you haven't yet caught him?' chided Hugo. 'I should have thought even Lestrade could have succeeded in such a case.'

'It's all very well for you to sneer,' grumbled Sinclair, 'but we're desperately under strength in the Met., and all this terrorism makes inordinate demands on manpower.'

'Yes, of course,' I soothed him, anxious not to spoil the snare I was confident I was laying for Hugo. 'These robberies — do they all follow the same pattern?'

'More or less. The perpetrator is a punk — in the sartorial sense, that is. He has a fan of pink hair running from the forehead to the nape of his neck, with the rest of the scalp shaven. He wears a black leather jacket and trousers, the latter being rather short for him, and both are decorated with chains and pins.

'His method is ludicrously simple. He marches into a shop, or office, where there are no more than one or two people, produces a gun and demands money. He rarely gets away with more than a few hundred, although once he was lucky enough to net over two thousand, but at an average of one hold-up a week he's doing quite nicely — and no income tax to pay! As soon as he's got the money, he orders his victims to turn round, roughly blindfolds them, ties their hands and makes off. He never bothers to make a really good job of immobilising his victims so they usually free themselves and raise the alarm quite quickly; but even so we've never so much as caught a glimpse of him ourselves. Once a constable was on the scene within two minutes of the offence taking place, but the criminal had apparently vanished without trace — or almost without trace.'

The detective smiled the smile of a small boy who had saved the best piece of cake until last.

'The oddest thing about it all is that the thief always leaves behind a new pair of size eleven boots.'

My first inclination was to burst out laughing, then I felt let down. Sinclair had been having us on and I was to be cheated of my test of Hugo's detective talent. However, the Inspector assured us that the facts as stated were quite genuine. He paused and sought solace in another drink.

'There, that's about all I can tell you of the case of what Dr. Watson might well have called The Adventure of the Vanishing Punk.'

'No other details?' enquired Hugo with unexpected seriousness. 'This man doesn't carry anything, a bag or something of that sort?'

'To put the swag in, you mean? No,

nothing of that kind. Some of those he's robbed say that he had a sort of yellowish cloth wrapped round his left arm, which he held across his body to rest the gun on. Of course, that means he's right-handed, but so are most people, so that observation doesn't get us very much further.'

'On the contrary,' smiled Hugo. 'The fulvous cloth is a most significant clue.'

Sinclair put down his drink.

'Really!' he remarked sarcastically. 'Have you solved the mystery? Shall we go and arrest the miscreant?'

Hugo ignored this sally.

'Were the Hare Krishna followers about on the days the robberies occurred?' he enquired inconsequentially.

'I suppose so,' shrugged the younger man. 'They're to be spotted almost every day up and down Oxford Street. People are so used to seeing them that nobody notices any more, except perhaps for the tourists. You're not really suggesting they have anything to do with it, are you?'

'No, but I think the gunman may have something to do with them.'

'But surely that comes to the same thing!' Sinclair exclaimed irritably.

'Not at all,' returned Hugo equably.

'Come on, Hugo,' I interrupted this pointless fencing. 'If you have an idea, let's hear it.'

'By all means. What is so striking about this punk robber?' he went on. 'Why, of course, his appearance — or rather, certain features of his appearance. Was anyone able clearly to describe his face, or help you with a photofit picture?'

'No,' admitted the policeman.

'I didn't think so. Their attention was naturally distracted by the striking hair-piece — and that, I suspect, is exactly what it was. Remove it, and there remains an ordinary-looking bald man, albeit in punk clothing. But now cover up those clothes with a rough yellowish robe (remember the too-short trousers?) and you have a punk no more, but a follower of Hare Krishna. Hence the perfunctory blindfolds to prevent any of the witnesses observing the transformation. The thief has only to slip out of the shop and along a probably-deserted street on to the main shopping thoroughfare, where he has ascertained a band of the followers of Krishna will be passing just then, and attach himself to the end of the line.

'Doubtless, too, he has sandals wrapped in the robe. His boots he is forced to abandon because of the difficulty of concealing them, and they will, as a result, be almost new each time.'

'Well, I'm damned!' profaned Sinclair. Then he laughed. 'It's certainly the kind of explanation Holmes would have deduced. But it won't do in real life. I can just imagine us arresting one of those Hare Krishna fellows and finding them quite innocent, and probably stark naked under their robes, too! 'Police Harassment of Religious Minority' — I can see the headlines now.'

'You needn't rush in, boots and all,' Hugo rebuked him. 'Use your intelligence. Have a plain clothes policeman watch the Hare Krishna band and, if an extra man comes out of a side street and joins them, that will be the one.'

'Very plausible, I'm sure,' chuckled Sinclair, not at all abashed. 'Come on. I'll allow you can make up fancy stories à la Conan Doyle, but leave real police work to the professionals.'

I don't think I've ever seen Hugo put out of countenance, but I'll swear he was somewhat miffed by Sinclair's attitude. As for me, I was convinced that Sinclair had made the whole thing up just to tease Hugo. I really couldn't swallow those abandoned boots! However, I had to admit to myself that Hugo had neatly turned the tables and explained everything to us with incontestable logic. Hugo obviously didn't share my suspicion of Sinclair's tale.

'Please yourself,' he shrugged, 'but I think you're overlooking a possibility.'

The Inspector regarded him thoughtfully for a while but said nothing more and we soon got on to talking about the effect of government cuts in University funding.

★ ★ ★

It must have been about a fortnight later that I came back to my office from lunch and found a note on my desk, from Helen Brown, the departmental secretary.

'Telephone Message.' I read. 'Hugo Lacklan says see today's Times, page 2. Helen. 1.15.'

I put the note on one side while I dealt with other matters, then went along to the Senior Common Room and found a copy of The Times. I turned to page two. It was only a small paragraph, but I spotted it almost immediately.

'Pink Punk Pinched', was the headline, and it went on:

'Police yesterday detained a man posing as a member of the Hare Krishna sect, but believed to be responsible for a series of daring robberies from small businesses in Soho and the environs of Oxford Street. The robberies were carried out by a man dressed as a punk, the thief then disguising himself as one of the religious musicians who regularly parade in Oxford Street, so making good his escape.'

I stared out of the large rain-speckled windows with unseeing eyes. Hugo's judgement was vindicated! My carefully-nurtured and heartfelt indifference to his previous expositions withered in the knowledge. In particular, if he was right about this, could I continue to ignore the implications of his explanation for the untimely demise of Magnus Thoren?

I shivered.

The Sound Of The Sea

I have to admit I was rather flattered when Carol Spence came to seek my assistance in the matter of the disappearance of Stephen Ennerdale. She is, after all, a remarkably attractive young lady, as well as being an extremely able student. My disillusionment was swift, however. It seems that my friend, Hugo Lacklan, has acquired something of a reputation in the academic community, not just as a notorious teller of tall tales, but as a sifter of real enigmas. I'm partly to blame, I suppose, having from time to time recounted some of his exploits.

His resolution of the riddle of *The Vanishing Punk* had, I will allow, made an impression upon me, and now I came to think of it, I believe I had regaled a number of research students with a perhaps exaggerated account of it, no doubt at tea one afternoon. Quite probably, Carol Spence would have been there.

Be that as it may, there is no denying that she was in a state of considerable distress when she appealed to me to enlist Hugo's aid and I found it quite impossible to refuse her entreaties, even though I was not at all sanguine either about interesting him in the problem or of his ability to resolve it.

In the end I telephoned the Department of Anthropology at the northern university which had the misfortune to count Hugo amongst its Professors and was lucky enough to catch him actually in his office working — a remarkable circumstance! I was not at all surprised to hear that he was paying one of his innumerable visits to the metropolis at the weekend. We arranged to meet on Saturday for lunch at The Lokanta Amasra, a Turkish restaurant off the Tottenham Court Road.

I took a slightly guilty pleasure in escorting Carol to the restaurant on the day and savoured Hugo's surprised appraisal. Carol seemed not to notice. Doubtless, she had become used to the effect her appearance had on the men she met.

We ordered kebab with salata and pilov,

followed by karpuz; a simple but satisfying meal. Hugo and I drank raki quenched with water, but Carol wisely stayed with gazoz. As we ate, Carol recounted the history of Stephen Ennerdale for Hugo's benefit.

The events pertinent to his disappearance began, it seemed, before he and Carol met, but Stephen had described to her how they came about and she remembered almost every word he spoke at the outset. Rendered in narrative form, his story was as follows.

★   ★   ★

Stephen Ennerdale sat alone on the sand. It was early April in Northumberland and the beaches of the north-east coast of England were deserted. Yet the sun was warm and the dunes behind gave shelter from the wind. He looked out over the sea. It was not rough, the breakers rolling lazily in, tumbling in a jumble of foam on the strand and hissing towards him only to be thwarted by the steeply sloping beach. Sun flashed on the breakers from the unsullied blue sky of the north.

He closed his eyes. The sun warmed his skin and the breeze caressed it. He listened to the sound of the sea. A wave rolled in and broke with muted thunder on the shore, swished across the sand then ran back murmuring to welcome the next. The sound beat upon him, insulating him, soothing him. He could sit for hours listening to the sea as it washed his mind free of the dross of city living. How healing it would be, he reflected, if he could listen to the sea every day instead of just a few days a year.

So was born the idea that lifted Stephen Ennerdale from his comfortable but mediocre existence to a state of luxury which was totally unexpected. It began when he bought a battery tape recorder and recorded a cassette full of the sound of the sea. That night in his lodging he played the tape back. It sounded shallow and metallic, but there was sufficient of the mesmeric force of the waves to encourage him to try again.

He returned the following year with more sophisticated equipment. At the end of the holiday, he did not feel as rested as he usually did. Juggling with microphones and recorders on the beach was not as relaxing as just sitting listening to the sea. The possibility of rain had disturbed him in a way it never had before; he worried about getting sand in everything and had to keep an eye on the sea lest it should creep up and drown his equipment. Nevertheless, as he drove south through the Tyne Tunnel and down the motorway, he felt satisfied that this time he had captured the authentic sound of the sea.

Stephen worked in London but could not afford to live close to his work, so each day he had a long journey home by underground and rail. On these journeys he tried to ignore the people around him, to shut out of his mind the noise and confusion and to fill it instead with the beating of waves on the shore. His home was a small but comfortable flat and, as soon as he got in on the first day after his holiday, he prepared and ate a filling albeit unnourishing meal.

At last he put on the tape of the sound of the sea, settled back in an armchair and closed his eyes as the sound washed over him, soothing yet stimulating. The room receded and he was back on the Northumbrian coast. The experience relaxed him but it also disturbed him, making him feel somehow lonely, as he sat in his flat listening to the sound of the distant ocean.

It was at a party he gave that Stephen first played the tape to anyone else. The party had been going some time and the flat was full of men and women talking and laughing, some shouting to be heard over the noise of the record player.

There was plenty to drink and not a great deal to eat, so that everyone was getting more and more excited. Seeing that they had all made themselves at home and were helping themselves to what or whom they needed, Stephen abandoned his role of host and managed to corner the girl who was the real reason for him throwing a party at all.

She worked in the same building and they had exchanged smiles but little else. He knew her name was Carol Spence, but there never seemed an opportunity to learn any more. Hence the party to which he had invited a number of people from work, including Carol.

Temporarily at a loss for conversation, he began telling her about his holiday. She was intrigued by the description of the tape he had made.

'Put it on now,' she begged. 'I'd love to hear it.'

Stephen was doubtful. It was part of his own private world and, while he would be only too pleased for Carol to share it, he had no wish for the rowdy party-makers around to laugh and scoff at it. However he gave in.

He slipped the cassette into the machine and, when the next record came to an end, he switched it on. Unwittingly, he had the volume up full and, without warning, the sound of the sea thundered through the flat. The roar of the surf drowned the babble of conversation, and the hiss of the dying wave silenced even the most determined conversationalist. Everyone stopped talking and looked towards the tape recorder and Stephen. Self-consciously, he turned the volume down.

'Sorry,' he muttered. 'I hadn't meant to have it so loud.'

'But it was gorgeous,' cooed a wide-eyed blonde. 'It went straight to my soul.'

'So does alcohol,' said her partner.

'You wouldn't recognise your own soul if it was labelled,' she retorted. 'Please, Stephen, turn it back up.'

There was a chorus of pleas and he complied.

'More!' somebody shouted and Stephen turned the volume up full.

The sound of the sea roared through the room, washing over the party-makers, calming and cleansing. Stephen was astonished at the effect. People who, a few minutes before had been chattering nineteen to the dozen, now sat silent, absorbed.

A faint ringing impinged annoyingly on Stephen's consciousness — the door bell. He hastened out into the hall.

It was the man from the flat below.

'I don't object,' began the man, 'to the sound itself. I've always liked the sea myself, but it is a bit loud, with the children in bed, too.'

'Of course,' apologised Stephen. 'I'll turn it down.'

But the sound was less compelling played softer.

'Look,' said somebody. 'My flat is in the attic of the building I live in and the flat below is empty, so there's nobody to disturb. Let's have another party there next weekend. Stephen can bring this tape along and we can play it as loudly as we like.'

So 'Sea Sound Parties' became a regular feature of Stephen's life, and so did Carol.

The parties got bigger and bigger. It was astonishing the effect which the amplified roar of the waves had on people. The sound of salt surf called to the pulse of salt blood in their veins and the listeners seemed to go into a trance, broken only by the end of the tape.

'Can't you make it into a loop so that it goes on and on for ever?' asked one girl.

After one of these sessions, Stephen found himself approached by a man who said his name was Johnny Josephson.

'I've a little bit of capital,' said

Josephson, 'and I've been looking for a way to make it into a big bit of income. I think you've found the way.'

'Oh?' Stephen said discouragingly.

'Yes. I expect to take a risk. You have to, to make money. But it's no good taking the kind of risk that's involved in backing a horse. The sort of risk I'm willing to take is backing my judgement about the sounds people will buy. I've been on the lookout for a new sound in the pop world, but there's nothing new there. Then I heard about your parties. Everybody who comes is wild about them and I can see why now. I think you've even temporarily unhooked a couple of junkies! They're hooked on your sea sound instead of the junk.'

'Do you mean to say,' Stephen queried doubtfully, 'that you think you could get people to pay money to listen to that tape?'

'Yes, in a way,' replied Josephson. 'I reckon, as a compact disc, that sound would sell a million. You can laugh if you like, but I'm telling you that sound is not just the sound that most people hear when they're close to the sea. Somehow, you've chosen to record a particular mood of the sea that bowls people over. And then the volume affects them, too. How many people can have heard the sea making that sort of noise? It's mind-stopping and people want their minds stopped. They don't like them running on, thinking, worrying, doubling. They want to be swept away, drowned in a 'sea' of sound. That tape releases them from themselves.'

'So, you want to make a record of the sea,' said Stephen. 'Why tell me?'

'Because you've already captured just the sound that's needed, on that tape. I'll buy it from you.'

'Do you really think you've a chance of making money with it?' asked Stephen, incredulously.

'I'll give you a hundred quid for the tape,' Josephson offered.

'You really must believe in it,' marvelled Stephen.

'Will you sell?' pressed Josephson.

'No. No, I won't,' came the reply, unexpected business acumen rising from

Stephen's subconscious. 'But I'll let you use it if you pay me royalties for every disc you sell.'

'Okay,' agreed Josephson. 'If that's the way you want it. I didn't think I'd convince you of the possibilities, otherwise I'd have suggested it straight off. It means a bit more capital conserved to finance the actual production.'

Thus *Sea Sounds* was founded.

Stephen had very little to do with it, apart from providing the tape, but Josephson seemed to know his way about. He had the tape transferred to disc and set about the promotion. It was slow work initially, but once it took hold, the demand rocketed and Josephson had difficulty contracting enough pressings. Cheques started to slip through Stephen's letter-box with numbing regularity and the figures on them soon became astonishing.

To begin with, the extra money made little difference to his way of life. He was able to buy more discs and books; he began to go out for his meals, especially with Carol. Then the company for which they both worked went into liquidation and together they were made redundant. Stephen found it didn't matter financially. The royalties from the disc were more than enough to make him independent. At first, it was difficult to adjust to his new freedom. The days seemed long and he felt uneasily that he was wasting them because he was no longer tied to an office routine.

Carol had decided to return to university life and work for a research degree. To start with, she was pleased about Stephen's economic freedom, but it soon produced strains. Stephen realised he was bored. If Carol gave up her new studies, they could spend their days together. He had more than enough money coming in for both of them. That, he was sure, would be much more fun. Carol was appalled by the suggestion. It offended her spirit of independence and she could never believe that the popularity of *Sea Sounds* would last; soon the bubble would burst. She urged Stephen to find a career. They quarrelled about it and so parted, Stephen sullen, Carol tearful.

His aimless way of life had infused

Stephen with lethargy. He made no attempt to renew his relationship with Carol and she was too proud to do so. She did not want to seem to be courting his money — money that had been too easily come by for her conscience. Besides, Stephen had been discovered by the media. Intent on exploiting the new cult of *Sea Sounds*, reporters interviewed him and television crews filmed him.

He became a celebrity.

His ordinariness, contrasting with his huge success, made him an irresistible attraction. He was introduced to an overwhelmingly new life-style, in which he drank too much, ate too much and found himself indulging in excesses of which he'd scarcely even day-dreamed.

One morning, he woke in his expensive new flat, for once alone. He felt terrible, but then he usually did in the mornings now. He moved unsteadily from the bedroom to the lounge and sank into an armchair. Mechanically, he switched on the radio. From it boomed the *Sound of the Sea* and he switched it off with a shudder. He had come to hate the recording which he heard everywhere, and which had changed his life so drastically. It no longer brought him release. He longed instead to recapture the original feeling he had enjoyed. Perhaps if he returned to Northumberland, to the real sea, he could regain some of that peace of mind he had experienced there so often before.

He stood up with new resolution. He quickly packed a few things in a bag and took a taxi to King's Cross station. While he waited for the next train north, he had some coffee and rolls and began to feel better.

The rhythm of the train beating its way the length of England lulled him and he slept soundly for the first time in months. When he woke, the train was nearing Newcastle where he had to change. It purred slowly across the bridge high above the Tyne and slid into the familiar cavernous station, where he transferred to a local service. When he reached the village, he automatically registered at the most expensive hotel rather than his former lodgings.

The next morning, he felt refreshed and ate a good breakfast before walking across the fields to the shore. The beach was deserted and curved away towards the low headland, where the gaunt black ruins of an ancient castle brooded over the jumble of rocks jutting into the sea.

He sat down on a rock and closed his eyes. The sea was in a gentle mood and the waves lapped at the beach, chasing the little pebbles along the strand with a quiet hiss. He listened and at first he thought it was going to work. He felt his mind begin to drift, but before he could lose himself in the soft sounds, he found his memory superimposing on the natural surf the sound of his recording, heard so often that every murmur was locked in his mind and with the remembered sound came all the associations he so wished to forget. His unsatisfying life washed about him like an unclean sea littered with the rubbish of a summer harbour and he was repelled.

Rising abruptly he walked away from the shore. He stared inland towards the distant hills. The country was empty and alone, but less so than he was himself. He had lost nirvana and might as well return to the world from which he had fled — but not yet. He would stay a few days. Perhaps after a week or so, he would go down to the beach again and see if he could yet recapture what he had thrown away.

Stephen hired a car and passed the days driving between the flower-strewn hedgerows of the long country lanes and up on to the empty moors, where the breeze carried the scent of bracken and the sound of sheep. He paused in the grey stone villages which seemed only half alive. From time to time, he would stop by the roadside to stretch his legs. It must have been on one of these occasions that he discovered a new way to cast off the moorings of his soul.

This was the brief history of Stephen Ennerdale and *Sea Sounds*, pieced together from Carol's account and from other information gleaned subsequently. For the latter months, after their parting, she had only gossip to go on and his final letter, in which he said how sorry he was to have spoilt the relationship they had had. He regretted that it seemed impossible to him that they could ever recapture their dreams. He was leaving London, thereby hoping to find the peace he once had enjoyed and then forfeited.

★   ★   ★

'Do you have the envelope?' interrupted Hugo, having listened in uncharacteristic silence to Carol's account thus far.
    'No, but it was posted at King's Cross,' she answered.
    'Did you try to trace him yourself?'
    She nodded.

★   ★   ★

As time passed, Carol had found her pride diminished by her longing once again to know Stephen's company. His face had disappeared from magazines and television with an abruptness which might have been astonishing if some new craze had not erupted to conceal the demise of the old. Perhaps, Carol thought, she and

51

Stephen could after all get back to where they were before *Sea Sounds* had driven them apart.

She knew the address of Stephen's new flat in London, although she had never been there. She felt a little intimidated as she took the aseptic lift to the top floor of the fashionable block which Stephen had chosen. She received a shock when she saw that the name on the door was not Stephen's, but she rang the bell nevertheless. A woman answered.

'Yes, dear?'

'I'm looking for Stephen Ennerdale.'

'Sorry, you've come to the wrong place, dear. He isn't one of mine.' The blowsy blonde frowned. 'Wait a minute, though. Wasn't that the name of the previous tenant? Yes, I'm sure it was. But he went ages ago.'

'Do you know where he went?' asked Carol.

'Haven't a clue, dear,' replied the woman.

Carol turned away bewildered. She realised that, despite his final letter, she had refused to believe that Stephen might not be there. The street suddenly seemed cold and unfriendly and she walked quickly to a nearby shopping centre, where she gratefully accepted the artificial cheerfulness of a coffee bar while she thought.

Who would know where Stephen was? If anyone, it would be Josephson, she reluctantly acknowledged — reluctantly because she disliked the man, regarding him as Stephen's evil genius. Carol nevertheless looked him up in a telephone book. She searched for Stephen's name too, but it was not there. She was not surprised: he'd never liked telephones. However, Josephson was in and she rang him. She asked him if he knew Stephen's new address.

★   ★   ★

'I feel certain he knew it,' Carol finished, as we drank our kahve, 'but he wouldn't tell me. I thought of going to see him, but — well, I know it's silly, but I just didn't feel up to it. He always gave me the creeps.'

She turned to Hugo.

'Could you help, please?' she pleaded. She need not have squandered her charm on Hugo Lacklan. I could see at a glance that he was intrigued by the problem.

'Yes, yes, of course,' he assured her. 'I'm sure there'll be no difficulty in getting the address. I've heard of Josephson and I know a thing or two about him. No; it isn't finding Ennerdale that will be interesting; the question is what will we discover when we visit him? What is he doing? That's what is so fascinating. Let's hope it's nothing so mundane as drugs or drink.'

On this unfeeling note, he turned and summoned the waiter, congratulating him in fluent Turkish on the excellence of the meal. The man beamed and shook our hands and urged us all — in idiomatic English — to come again.

It was almost a week later, Friday afternoon to be exact, when I heard from Hugo again. I was sitting musing in my office in the Chemistry Department, trying to mark examination scripts. Instead, I was finding my eyes drawn irresistibly to the dazzling cumulus towering in the blue sky visible from my windows. My room is high on the corner of the building, with floor-to-ceiling windows on the south and west sides, so that it catches the afternoon sun and induces a pleasant somnolence, especially on Fridays!

The telephone penetrated my torpor and reluctantly I answered. It was Hugo to say that he had acquired Ennerdale's new address and could Miss Spence and I travel north tomorrow? He promised to meet us at Newcastle and said his College could put us up for a couple of nights. I told him that I would check with Carol and ring him back.

I descended several flights of stairs to the research laboratory where the girl worked, and found her examining thin-layer chromatography plates under ultra-violet light. She was attempting to separate some rather interesting synthetic analogues of the cytochromes. We fell to discussing a recent paper on biosynthetic routes to porphyrin rings in general and I almost forgot my purpose in seeking her out. However when Carol learned of Hugo's success, she was very eager to accept his invitation.

As we drove south from Newcastle Central Station through Gateshead towards the motorway and the ancient fortress where the more fortunate members of Hugo's college had their rooms, he regaled us with an account of his encounter with Josephson.

'We met in a pub in an alleyway off Cheapside. I'd inveigled him along by the infallible expedient of professing myself interested in investing money in one of his enterprises. In view of Carol's experience with the man, I didn't immediately ask him for Ennerdale's address. Instead, I related the curious affair of the disappearing punk to him, embroidering it slightly, and making a great deal of my friendship with Inspector Sebastian Sinclair. He gave me some old-fashioned looks but I was undeterred.

'Then I made a few pointed remarks about poor Thoren's ill-fated brother and his drug-induced demise. I could see this really rattled him. However, Josephson is no fool and as soon as I let out that I was interested in discovering Ennerdale's present where-abouts, he relaxed some-what but nevertheless told me what he knew.

''You know where he's living,' I persisted.

''Yes, I do,' Josephson said, 'but I wouldn't advise you to contact him. He's become very strange.'

''What do you mean?' I asked.

''Well,' replied Josephson slowly, 'when the *Sea Sounds* thing started to die, I thought I'd ask Stephen if he had any more ideas. It was then I realised he'd faded from the scene. I managed to trace him to a place in Northumberland, a biggish house called Crag Hall. I went up to see him. It was the depth of winter and Crag Hall was miles from anywhere, it may even have been over the Scottish border. Stephen seemed neither pleased nor displeased to see me; he was in some way remote. I just couldn't get through to him. If I weren't so familiar with the minor symptoms of drug addiction, I'd have said he was stoned but it definitely wasn't that. I broached the idea of a follow-up to *Sea Sounds*. He wasn't interested. He said he didn't need any more money. *Sea Sounds* had made him enough. Now he simply wanted to be left alone.'

' 'Perhaps it was just you he wasn't anxious to see again,' I suggested.

'Josephson laughed. He had gained the impression that it would have made no difference to Ennerdale who his visitor was. He had no wish to see anyone.

'As he left, Ennerdale had watched Josephson until he had turned out of the drive, as though making sure that he really was leaving. The blank expression on his face had not flickered even for a moment.'

★　★　★

The next morning, Hugo drove us north at an even pace in his Rover. Carol occupied the front passenger seat and I lounged in the back. None of us was inclined to speculate on what we might find and Hugo filled the silence with cassettes of the guitar music of Barrios, the great Paraguayan composer of part Indian descent..

With the urban tangle of Gateshead and Newcastle behind us, we quickly reached Morpeth and took the Coldstream road along the edge of the swelling Cheviots. The northern sun was surprisingly warm and the verges were dotted with spring flowers. Yet in the distance, the hills brooded darkly, hinting at hidden places and enigmatic peoples.

North of Wooler, we followed a lane westward to Kirknewton, a name loaded with a sense of overwhelming personal loss for me and I was glad that I was alone in the back of the car as we drove by the hamlet. We were following the signs for Yetholm and Morebattle, deep into the secret heart of the hills. Hugo needed no map: he knew these roads well. Even so, he slowed down after we crossed the Scottish border, hunting the turn he knew must come soon. When he found it, it was barely large enough for the big car and bushes caught at us as we passed. Eventually, we came to an open gate in the high hedge. Hugo swung the car carefully into the driveway and stopped.

A wild and unkempt garden stretched up towards a large and forbidding house. Beyond it towered a group of sparse pines and beyond them loomed the crag which gave the house its name. The air was still and very quiet.

We got out of the vehicle and walked in silence up to the front door. Carol pressed the bell, but there was no sound. Nobody came. She tried the knocker, but there was no response. Without a word, Hugo set off along the front of the house. We followed him round the corner. As we approached the back, we heard the whispering of wind in the pines.

The whispering grew louder and I stopped stock still, gazing at the firs. They were unmoving. There was no wind to disturb them, yet I could hear it plainly, the restless susurration of a wind tugging at twigs and branches, rising and falling, bathing my mind in the indescribable experience of nature. I glanced at Carol and her puzzled expression told me she heard it too. We worked our way round until we found ourselves on a raised terrace, its stones overrun with weeds. The sound of the wind was much louder now and seemed, surprisingly, to originate from within the house.

Large windows overlooked the terrace. We went up to one and peered through the Georgian panes. In the centre of the room, I could see Stephen Ennerdale reclining in an armchair, his eyes closed, and an expression of deep peace on his face. By his side was a recording machine and it was from this that there emanated the whispering, roaring, caressing, searching sound of the wild wind in the pines.

★   ★   ★

There's little more to tell. We left as silently as we had come and Hugo drove us to Wooler, where we found a tea shop. Hot coffee dispelled the blanket of silence which had enfolded us. Having found Stephen Ennerdale and having discovered his secret addiction to the new sound that had taken over his life, Hugo and I felt there was nothing more we could do.

Carol agreed. She was effusive in her thanks to Hugo.

We returned to London together, but a week later Carol took a fortnight's leave. How she weaned Stephen from his introspection I don't know, but she is a determined as well as a beautiful woman and had she fastened her attentions on me I have not the slightest doubt I would have found them totally irresistible! In any event she succeeded and some while later I met the pair of them.

I would hardly have recognised him as the unshaven and unkempt refugee from reality slumped in that chair between the quadraphonic speakers in Crag Hall. As for Carol, she looked radiant and more beautiful than ever.

The Expensive Daub

Not far from the College of which I am a fellow, there exists a small gallery owned by two brothers. They have another, larger establishment somewhere in the region of New Bond Street. The younger of the two Grodzinskis runs the West End gallery, and no doubt that is where they make their money, for the works exhibited by the elder brother in the rooms off Rope Passage are all modestly priced, and even so I imagine sales are few and far between, although Lionel Grodzinski never seems perturbed.

'If a few kids come in off the street to look around, and go out with a new slant on life, I feel better than if I'd sold a Matisse to some grasping collector who sees not a picture but an investment,' he once said to me.

One lunchtime, having spent the morning covering blackboards with mathematical derivations of second order rate equations, and the conclusions to be drawn from Arrhenius factor values, activation energies and other arcana of chemical kinetics, I felt the need to refresh myself with something different, so I strolled down the main road and turned into Rope Passage.

The noise of traffic was instantly diminished, and the tall buildings shaded the narrow alleyway from the hot sun. I went into the gallery through the door between Sita Wholesale and Luigi's Trattoria, and climbed the stairs. Lionel Grodzinski smiled at me and gestured with his palms open, his shoulders lifting as though to both welcome me and encourage me to look round. I wandered through the four small second floor rooms where canvasses, mainly by local artists, were displayed. Although Grodzinski was eager to encourage new painters, he never allowed his enthusiasm to cloud his judgement. Not everything he showed was to my own taste, but I could always see why he had found it acceptable. I was astonished, therefore, on that particular day, to come across a blotchy abstract of no discernible merit whatsoever, and carrying a truly astonishing price tag furthermore. While I stood looking at this repulsive exhibit, Lionel Grodzinski joined me.

'What do you think of it?' he asked, indicating the object of my displeasure.

'It's awful,' I replied. 'What on earth made you hang it, and the price — is it a joke?'

Grodzinski shook his head deprecatingly.

'No! No, indeed not.' He sighed. 'It's the work of an artist, no longer quite young, who clearly has very little talent.'

'And you are sorry for him?'

'Again, no; in fact, I rather dislike him.'

'Then why stick the fellow's work on your wall? Unless it is to make the other works shine by comparison!'

'Please, Dr. Dunkley, you know me better than that.'

'I thought I did, but seeing this abomination makes me wonder!'

I smilingly relented.

'No, of course I don't think so ill of you, it's just that I am at a loss for an explanation.'

'My brother persuaded me. You are a practical man, Dr.Dunkley, a man of science, but a practical man nonetheless.'

(Lionel Grodzinski likes his little jokes).

'I am sure,' he went on, 'that you will realise we make very little money from this gallery. From the West End establishment, yes, we do well enough, but here it is a different story. But we like to think we are doing something for others here; it's a kind of service to struggling artists, and to local people who might otherwise never come in contact with art at all. It is if you like our sacrifice to the gods for our good fortune.

'Recently, however, the other gallery has not been doing so good, and we began to think that we might not be able to continue here as well.'

Grodzinski paused while we moved into an adjoining room. The whole of one wall of this was dominated by a painting of a brown car against a mauve background.

'What do you think of that?' he asked me.

'It's impressive. I don't like it, wouldn't buy it, because I couldn't live with it, but there's no denying its impact. It is quite sinister, and I'm not sure why. The composition itself contains no overtly threatening images; I think it must be the combination of colours that is so menacing.'

Lionel nodded.

'The woman who painted that has talent. Yet she'll be lucky to get the sixty guineas she's asking, whereas that daub we've just left will make two hundred pounds without any difficulty.'

'How can you be so sure?'

'I've already sold two similar canvasses for just that sum.'

I was astonished.

'I still don't quite know why I took the first one,' went on the gallery owner. 'This man came in one day; said his name was Cavan and he was down to his last crust, would I sell a painting for him? I said I'd look at his work.

'He had a canvas with him; it was dreadful. He claimed he'd already sold several through another gallery, but they'd decided to concentrate on 19th century artists, so he was now looking for a new opportunity. He . . . Well, never mind how he talked me into it, I'm still not sure to this day. When he told me what he wanted for it. I didn't even argue.

'A week later a tall distinguished-looking foreigner came into the gallery and, after perusing everything, bought Cavan's picture.'

'And was it as over-priced as this one?'

'Any price would be too much for something like that, but yes, it was two hundred, and the buyer didn't even haggle.

'Three days afterwards, Cavan came into the Gallery again, saw his picture had gone, and so collected his money. He was back the next day, with another piece just like it.'

Grodzinski sighed.

'I ought to have refused it; it was worthless. Yet I began to have twinges of doubt. Could there, I asked myself, be some merit in the work that I could not discern? So the opportunity to reject it passed; Cavan had gone, leaving the ghastly daub behind. Within a week, the mysterious buyer was back, and again he bought the Cavan. He purchased a couple of other canvases, too, but it was obvious it was the Cavan he valued. So here I am with a third of the things on my wall, waiting around to see if the foreign buyer will take this one too.'

Several weeks passed before I looked in at the gallery again. Grodzinski told me that the third Cavan had been purchased by the same man as the others and there was now a fourth on his walls. I stared at it, but failed to convince myself it was anything other than repulsive.

★   ★   ★

That weekend, Hugo Lacklan was down in London, to give a lecture at the Royal Institution. On an impulse, I took him along to the gallery, and persuaded Lionel Grodzinski to retell the story of the paintings, knowing how Hugo relishes any example of the quirkiness of human nature. I was quite gratified by the rapt attention with which Hugo listened to the tale, and surprised by the time he spent almost motionless in front of the canvas itself. At length, he stirred.

'I'll take it,' he said.

I was astounded.

'You can't really want it!' I expostulated.

'Oh, but I do, I think it will be a good investment.'

'Really, Dr. Lacklan, I could not recommend it,' advised Grodzinski. 'If you seriously wish to invest in art, you should visit our other gallery or if you want to back an unknown who may one day be valuable, there are several here I could put forward; but this — this is nothing; worse than nothing, it is worth less than unsullied canvas.'

'The mysterious buyer doesn't think that.'

'Ah-ha!' I interrupted. 'You scent a mystery, Hugo. You think there is more to this than an eccentric collector.'

'Perhaps. Come, Mr. Grodzinski. Will you sell to me rather than your regular customer?'

'Well, if you are determined, why should I resist further? Just as long as it is quite understood that it is against my professional advice.'

'Perfectly.'

As we walked to the nearby underground station, past the stalls of the local street market, I questioned Hugo closely about his purchase.

'You suspect some jiggery-pokery in connection with these pictures,' I accused him. 'Well, I think you are going to come a cropper this time, and an expensive one, too. Just because you were lucky over that business of the disappearing punk, you imagine you are some sort of detective.'

Hugo smiled, in a rather infuriating way.

'I certainly wouldn't lay claims to any such thing in this connection. It is quite obvious what is going on, at least in outline.'

We descended the steps to the station, and boarded a Metropolitan Line train. Before we parted at the Barbican, Hugo said:

'Pop in and see me tomorrow, if you have time, and I think I'll be able to surprise you.'

I seldom go up to town on a Sunday, but Hugo's invitation was irresistible, so when I should have been working at home, I was instead in a lift rising almost to the top of one of those pleasingly involuted towers that grace The Barbican Centre, where Hugo has an almost penthouse flat. Don't ask me how he afforded it, because I don't know. He certainly couldn't do it on his salary alone, but perhaps he has some lucrative consultancies. I suppose someone, somewhere, must have a commercial need for anthropology. Once upon a time, Hugo used to stay at the rooms belonging to The Royal Anthropological Society on his frequent visits to London, but after he was expelled from the Society he was naturally declared *persona non grata* there. Hence his decision to buy a pied à terre.

Hugo greeted me with his customary affability.

'Have a glass of mead,' he proffered. I accepted gratefully.

'From Holy Island?'

'No. The local supermarket has it now.

Of course, it is very convenient to be able to buy anything you can afford wherever you are, but it has taken some of the pleasure out of travelling; aeroplanes have removed the rest.'

'Now, then,' he went on. 'Come and have a look at this.'

He led me into an adjoining room and indicated an easel set in the middle of it. On this was a painting which looked to me like a very good copy of a pointillist canvas by Seurat. I said as much to Hugo.

'It may look like a good copy to you,' he rejoined. 'To me, it looks like the real thing.'

'You're not serious!'

'Perfectly. How much do you think it cost me?'

'Two hundred pounds!' I answered without the slightest hesitation.

'Exactly,' Hugo nodded approvingly. 'I had a friend of mine from The Courtauld Galleries come over yesterday evening and clean those horrid colours off that canvas I bought, and this was underneath.'

'And he agrees it's genuine?'

'He thinks it very likely, though like all these fellows he's cautious. But, after all, if it were a copy, why cover it over? What's more, it's a painting that has been missing for over two years, stolen from a private collection.'

'And you guessed this when you offered to buy it from old Grodzinski?'

'I had an inkling that something like this was the explanation for the story he told us. It seems to be a neat way of smuggling stolen works of art out of the country. A foreign buyer comes over here, takes back a number of canvasses by unknown artists, and concealed under the paint of one of them, or possibly of more, is a Seurat or a Sisley.'

It really seemed as though Hugo had once again stumbled on some odd occurrence, and with that sharp and eccentric mind of his had somehow discerned the truth underlying it.

However, that was not the whole story. On Monday, I was struggling with the draft of a review I was writing on the use of copper reagents in synthetic organic chemistry, when the telephone rang. It was Hugo, and he sounded far from his ebullient self.

'That Seurat was a fake!' he announced without preamble, and there was a depth of indignation in his voice which brought an unsympathetic grin to my lips. Fate, it seemed, had at last pulled the rug out from under Hugo's feet.

'I took the canvas round to the Courtauld Institute,' he went on, 'and James gave it the works; it's a very good forgery, but forgery he's convinced it is.'

'So you're somewhat out of pocket,' I gibed unfeelingly.

'Hardly that. As a copy, it's good enough to be worth what I paid for it.'

'That good?'

'Oh yes. But it isn't the money that bothers me. It's the fact that I was wrong! And even more infuriating, I just don't understand what's going on! Something obviously is. No one paints a beautiful reproduction, and then daubs paint all over it in such a ghastly way just to take the thing out of the country. There's no need to smuggle copies!'

'What are you going to do now?'

I felt sure Hugo would have some plan in mind. He isn't the sort to admit defeat, still less to telephone to announce it.

'James had photographed the daub before he cleaned it off. He's going to repaint it. I'm certain that the foreign buyer will be calling in at the Gallery, expecting the painting to be there. I've told Grodzinski to allow himself to be persuaded to give the man my address. I expect to receive a visit from him before long.'

After Hugo had rung off, I returned to my review, but try as I might I couldn't concentrate on my work at all. I kept turning over in my mind the strange business of the expensive daub.

The following Thursday, I was home late, having been playing chess for the local club side. I was in a good mood, elated at having won an intricate game resulting from my own offer of the Queen's Gambit, to which my opponent had replied with the King's Indian Defence. The telephone began to ring almost as soon as I was through the door. It was Hugo.

'I was right,' he announced, and rushed on before I had a chance to make any barbed comments. 'The mysterious buyer came tonight. He offered me three-fifty for the picture.'

'Three pounds fifty pence?' I enquired derisively.

'Three hundred and fifty pounds,' returned Hugo, in the tones of one lecturing to a class of idiots. 'Something is definitely going on. He bribed Grodzinski to the tune of one hundred just for my address, and promised him an under-the-counter commission if he ensured that he got first refusal when the next canvas came on the market.'

'So Grodzinski now knows who the man is?'

'No. He said he would contact Grodzinski from time to time, and to hold on to any canvasses from Cavan until he heard.'

'Well,' I remarked, 'apart from being one hundred up on the transaction, I can't see that you are any further forward.'

'Patience, Alex, patience. Old Grodzinski tells me that Cavan always calls in for the proceeds of a sale within two or three days. He doesn't know how Cavan is so quick off the mark, but it seems clear to me that the buyer must notify Cavan that he has made a collection. In fact, the whole thing seems quite transparent now that I've had time to think it over. There is only one logical explanation. Anyway, I'm going to be spending the next few days in the stock room behind Grodzinski's office. When Cavan comes in, I shall follow him.'

'Hm! Do you really think you'll be able to?'

Hugo assumed an injured tone.

'You're forgetting my splendid performance in the enigma of The Five Elderly Gentlemen.'

'That was different. Cavan may well be a professional villain if, by any chance, the suspicions you hint at are well-founded.'

Several more days passed before Hugo once again telephoned me at work.

'Meet me outside Stepney Green underground station in half-an-hour,' he commanded, silencing my protests of pressing work to do, with a peremptory challenge as to whether or not I wanted to unravel the mystery of the valuable fake.

It was raining as we emerged together from the station, having met by the newsagents in the booking hall. Hugo guided us left into Globe Road and then through the several small roads of a complex of flats and elderly houses, many of them renovated and looking in better condition than the decaying tower blocks. We went into a pub, not one of the old, established hostelries of the area, but a new one evidently intended to be a local for the housing estate. It looked as though it had failed to catch on and I wasn't surprised. Inside, it was spick, span and cheerless. Hugo secured pints of beer, and steered me to a table in a corner, at which a solitary man sat. He looked up as we approached, obviously startled, as well he might be, since there were only two other people in the bar, and dozens of unoccupied tables.

'Good evening, Mr. Cavan,' Hugo started, pleasantly enough, as we sat down at the man's table without asking his permission.

'Who the hell are you?' demanded the artist.

'Who I am is of no consequence, beside the fact that I know about your little game.'

'What do you mean?'

'You're a very good painter,' remarked Hugo, 'or at any rate copyist. It's a pity you have to cover such craftsmanship with blotchy rubbish that isn't worth the cost of the paints used.'

'I don't know what you mean, and I don't want to hear any more of it. Push off, before I get the landlord to throw you out.' Hugo sighed.

'That sort of attitude isn't going to help keep your secret, is it? You've heard of Inspector Sebastian Sinclair, perhaps?'

The man's expression showed he had.

'I thought so; this used to be his manor, I believe. He's an old student of mine,'

'Student?' Cavan said incredulously. 'You mean you teach rozzers? Strewth, whatever next? What do you want? I

80

haven't done anything illegal. There's nothing you can touch me for.'

'That's my understanding of the matter, certainly,' answered Hugo soothingly, 'but there are one or two details I want to iron out, just to make sure that this is something Sebastian need not be bothered with.'

Little by little, using a judicious mixture of guile, flattery and intimations of unpleasant consequences, and aided by the purchase of several rounds of drinks, Hugo extracted the details of the dubious enterprise in which Cavan and his continental associate were engaged.

By the time the tale was told, it was dark outside. Hugo and I made our way carefully through the balmy air, back to Stepney Green station, Hugo chuckling quietly to himself all the way. Once ensconced in a brightly-lit train, heading westward, he burst into outright laughter, causing an elderly lady to retreat to the far end of the carriage.

'I'm glad you find it so hilarious,' I interrupted his jollity somewhat acidly, 'and I agree it has its amusing aspects,

81

but it seems to me at least immoral, even if it isn't illegal, and I'm not entirely convinced on that latter point, either.'

'My dear chap,' responded Hugo, 'you are of course right on both points — it is immoral, and it is most probably illegal in some way or other, but when friend Cavan said 'there's nothing you can touch me for', I suspect he was right. In practical terms, prosecution would be out of the question. And I for one am gratified.'

★ ★ ★

The scheme which Cavan had revealed to us — or, as Hugo maintained, confirmed for him — was an impudent one.

Cavan had compiled a list going back a good many years, of valuable works of art stolen and never recovered. Once they had been missing for two years, he reckoned that they were gone for good, probably into the collection of some wealthy but unscrupulous collector, who would gloat over them in secret, but be unable ever to acknowledge their acquisition. Satisfied on this point, Cavan would then paint an imitation of the masterpiece, using published reproductions as a guide, and following a careful study of the artist's technique as discernible in other paintings exhibited in public galleries. Cavan was indeed a master craftsman, a forger par excellence, as Hugo's friend from the Courtauld had testified.

When the painting was ready, Cavan's accomplice would find a buyer, any of those dubious collectors who were willing to buy stolen works of art, with very few questions asked. The pictures were never offered at home, always abroad. The final conviction of authenticity was provided by the smuggling of the counterfeit masterpiece out of England, hidden beneath an atrocious piece of slap-stick. Even allowing for various expenses, the profits on these deals must have been very considerable.

'Consider,' remarked Hugo, 'who loses? Only the final buyer of the work, someone who is quite willing to accept property stolen from its rightful owner. Should we feel any sympathy for such a person? Surely not. As well as themselves being no better than a common fence, they have no compunction in denying enjoyment by the world at large of a work they believe genuine, putting their own pleasure at a premium far in excess of that of their fellow men.

'No, I'm glad they are being duped. The only sorrow need be that they don't know it! And you must admire the audacity and simplicity of the scheme. Suppose the courier is caught taking the picture out of the country. Of what crime will he be guilty? None! It is after all, merely a copy. Supposing the purchaser discovers it is a fake, what can he do about it? Very little. He certainly couldn't alert the police without exposing himself to investigation, censure and a possible charge of intent to purchase stolen property. He might employ thugs to intimidate Cavan and the intermediary — if he can find them. No, all in all, I regard it as an admirable enterprise — the exploitation of the avarice and egotism of the very rich!'

I had to admit that, put like that, it seemed almost a public service!

The Man Who Wrote Letters

The Law of Cause and Effect is perhaps no more than a restatement in scientific terms of the platitudinous saying that one thing leads to another. So far as Hugo Lacklan's resolution of enigmas was concerned it certainly seemed to be true. If he had advertised himself as an investigator of bizarre occurrences I'm sure he could have been no more successful in attracting pleas for help. The matter of Carol Ennerdale's aunt is a case in point. It arose from Hugo's involvement in the strange disappearance of Stephen Ennerdale, in which Carol Spence, as she then was, appealed to Hugo for his assistance, having heard me mention his elucidation of the curious matter of the Vanishing Punk — yet another example of one thing leading to another.

I must stick to one story at a time, however. I don't ramble when I'm drafting a paper for the Journal of the Chemical Society, but somehow I never know quite how to begin these accounts of Hugo's exploits. Perhaps I should start with Hugo's telephone summons to me to meet him within the hour in the coffee bar of Camden Library in Euston Road. Whether he was combining a professional visit to the library with his patronage of its coffee bar I never discovered, but it seems unlikely as Camden Public Library is hardly renowned for its stock of anthropological material.

When we were settled comfortably with our coffee, I pressed Hugo for an explanation.

'What are you doing in London this time?' I began.

'Oh, this and that,' he replied evasively.

'And is it this or that about which you wish to talk to me?' I enquired sarcastically.

Hugo grinned.

'You remember Carol Ennerdale?'

Of course I did. Besides being an

excellent scientist and an outstandingly beautiful woman, she had insisted that both Hugo and I attend her wedding to Stephen, on the grounds that without us it might never have occurred and so we ought to feel some responsibility.

'I had a letter from her,' continued Hugo.

'I hope nothing is wrong. Stephen hasn't shown any — well sign of — well you know what I mean?' I questioned, anxiously and rather incoherently.

'Oh no,' Hugo reassured me. 'Everything is fine with Stephen and Carol Ennerdale, but she wondered if I might be interested in a somewhat odd occurrence affecting a middle-aged aunt of hers.'

It was my turn to smile.

'When she says 'interested in' I take it she means there is some mystery she thinks you'll be able to solve.'

'That was indeed her hope,' he agreed.

'And you are flattered and intrigued!'

'I'll admit the affair has its singular aspects. Briefly, the facts are as follows. Carol's aunt, Miss Ophelia Spence, is a lady of middle years whose unmarried state Carol attributes to her unselfish care of old Mrs. Spence, since Miss Ophelia is apparently by no means unprepossessing even now and in her youth must have been pretty, if not beautiful. Furthermore she is of a sunny and outgoing nature.'

'You have met the lady yourself or are you relying solely on Carol's assessment?'

'I have visited Miss Spence. She lives in a neat solid bungalow in the small village of Hampton Poyle near Oxford. It has an exquisite church, incidentally, and I can recommend a visit. She was apologetic at being the cause of my journey but I assured her that I was in her debt on account of the church, and the hauntingly picturesque ruins of a Jacobean house I came across in ambling through the fields beyond the hamlet.'

I must I think, have given some sign of impatience at this lengthy discursion, since Hugo abruptly returned to the point.

'I won't bore you with a sentence by sentence account of our conversation;

what it amounted to was this. Although content enough in the bungalow she had purchased after the death of her mother, and finding great solace in gardening and exercise in walking, she nevertheless felt in need of something out of the ordinary, some hint of spice in her life which participation in village and church affairs did not provide. It was for this reason that an advertisement in one of those magazines still so popular with women of all ages — you know the sort: romantic stories, recipes, readers' letters, comforting thoughts, hints on appearance and so on — caught her attention. It offered simply a pen-friend service. It would put applicants in touch with someone of the opposite sex matching their requirements but it was not, and this was very strongly emphasised, a matrimonial bureau. Indeed applicants were asked to abjure any intention of cultivating a closer relationship than that of correspondents.'

'That seems a little puritanical,' I remarked.

'The proprietor of the bureau, in the letter sent to Miss Spence as a result of her enquiry, pointed out that there already existed many bureaus dedicated to effecting introductions with prospects of marriage — or other liaisons — in mind, and that this was not the purpose of his own organisation. He offered a marriage of minds perhaps, but nothing more. It was a romantic notion which appealed strongly to Miss Spence, and doubtless others of her ilk. She duly completed the form, listing her interests and personal — but not too personal — particulars. She sent it to the bureau — a box number, which is not uncommon I think — together with the modest fee requested. She received a reply sooner than she expected, from a gentleman signing himself simply 'Donald'. There was no address — this being one of the rules of the organisation, supposedly to guard against unforeseen consequences which might redound to the disrepute of the bureau.

'Miss Spence and Donald soon struck up a genuine friendship by correspondence. They had a lot in common, as was to be expected, but more than that they seemed really to be of one mind about a great many things, yet each was able to enrich the other with knowledge and insights that were new. They fell into the habit of writing to each other — always via the bureau's box number — once a week and Miss Ophelia found it gave her that little thrill of expectation which enhanced but did not threaten her even existence. They exchanged photographs and Miss Spence was gratified to find her correspondent to be a very distinguished looking gentleman, while he in turn complimented her on her appearance.

'This agreeable arrangement might have continued undisturbed, were it not for one of those freakish pranks that fate delights in playing. Needing to travel up to London on business, Miss Spence took a bus into Oxford, intending to catch a mid-morning train. It was late in arriving and to while away the time she bought a woman's magazine. It contained a number of sentimental stories, including one by the well known writer Deidre Forsyth, which struck a particular chord in Miss Spence. It concerned a lady of middle years, whose life in many ways resembled her own. So intrigued was she by it, that she read it several times and each time noticed fresh similarities so that before long she quite identified with the character. The woman in the story had for long corresponded with a man she had known more or less since childhood, who had emigrated to Canada. This indeed was different from Miss Spence's experience and so too was the conclusion of the story for, almost inevitably in such a magazine, the man returned unexpectedly to England, the two arranged to meet and romance blossomed.

'Until she read this simple tale, Miss Spence had imagined herself quite content with her existence but suddenly she began to feel less so. She started to question her assumption that her role in life had been determined once and for all when she took responsibility for the care of her aging parent, and to wonder if it really were inevitable that she should die a 'maiden aunt'.

'Once this notion germinated, Aunt Ophelia found herself unable to root it out. It grew at the expense of her former content. Her new aspiration inevitably focussed on the person of her correspondent, in contravention of the bureau's code but what did that matter? She and Donald were individuals not marionettes. What they did was up to them and rereading his letters she persuaded herself that there were indications that he was not indifferent to the possibility of a warmer relationship than that offered by pen and paper. Phrases that she had taken as conventional compliments might be interpreted as conveying real feeling. If Donald nurtured any desire to meet her, why should it not be fulfilled? The suggestion, she felt, must come from her since she was sure he would regard it as unfair for him to propose varying the rules under which they had been introduced.

'So she wrote to him, remarking on the length of their correspondence and how well she felt they had come to know each other. She ended by admitting that if he felt that a meeting would not upset their friendship, then she would be happy to agree.

'She anticipated that he might well demur; that his own life might admit of no more than the relationship as it stood; but she was startled by the reply she received. It was not unpleasant or even discourteous; it was not irritated or injured; no, the impression it conveyed to her was one almost of panic. He seemed to hint that some terrible calamity might occur were she to persist. She wrote back immediately assuring Donald that she would do nothing to alter the status quo and waited anxiously for his reply. Instead she received a type-written note from the bureau stating that they had been informed by a close relative of Donald, that he had died suddenly and unexpectedly and offering Miss Spence sympathy at this unhappy termination of their correspondence.

'Miss Spence found it difficult to accept this statement as true. It was too much of a coincidence — the hint of disastrous consequences, the sudden demise. It seemed to her only too likely it was a subterfuge to break their relationship irrevocably.

'Of course she was upset but then with the resolution gained through many years of caring for a loved but often exasperating and finally senile parent, she endeavoured to put the whole experience behind her and to fill the gap it had left with new interests. Ultimately she failed and was honest enough to admit it to herself. There seemed to her to be only one way to lay the ghost of the once vital though distant, relationship she had enjoyed. She must find out exactly why Donald was so shaken by her suggestion of a meeting and whether he really had died or was shamming or if indeed, she suggested diffidently, some more sinister reason did lie behind it all. She realises that the most likely explanation is that he is happily married and wanted only the pleasure of correspondence as advertised by the bureau. Nevertheless, something in his letters convinced her that it was otherwise, that he would never have sunk to the deception this presupposed, and knowing of the help we had given Carol after Stephen disappeared she asked Carol to consult us once more.'

This sudden switch from the first person singular to the first person plural was a clear warning to me that Hugo was planning to involve me in some way and I ought to have refused to become embroiled without more ado, as my time was already heavily committed; but the enigma of Miss Ophelia's Donald had already taken hold and I weakly succumbed to Hugo's snare.

'Miss Spence is unable to rid herself of the worry that Donald may be trapped in some situation repugnant to him but from which he cannot escape and she is determined to discover whether this is so and, if it is, to do her best to free him. However all her communications with him had been via the bureau and there were no real clues in Donald's letters as to where he lived. His occupation, which he had described as a freelance buyer for the better class antiques trade, took him all over the country and while he often wrote of the places he visited he never spoke of anywhere as home.'

Intrigued though I was, I felt distinctly chary of becoming enmeshed in anything of a deeply personal nature, and I said so.

'I am entirely in agreement with you,' answered Hugo irrepressibly. 'I have no intention of playing an agony uncle. But having seen some of Donald's letters, including the most recent, I share Miss Spence's suspicions.'

'So what are you going to do? Surely St. Catherine's House would . . . but no, without a surname it would be impossible. I suppose the bureau won't give you any assistance?'

'The magazine refused to reveal the address of the bureau and I doubt whether a letter via the box office number would elicit any response other than a reiteration of Donald's supposed demise. However, we have a clue!'

With this rather dramatic announcement, Hugo took from the inside pocket of his jacket, a brown envelope from which he extracted a photograph. He handed it to me without comment as though challenging me to deduce something from it. It was the portrait of a man, taken out of doors. I turned it over. On the back was written: *With kindest regards, Donald.*

As this evidently was a picture of Miss Spence's pen-friend I looked at it again. The figure was not posed but had been snapped in the act of strolling along what looked like a promenade. He was obviously approaching the photographer, so that both railings and the beach and a glimpse of sea were visible on the left, while to the right was a roadway.

'It looks like the sort of snap a seaside photographer might take,' I ventured.

'Bravo,' cried Hugo. 'Just my thought.'

'But I don't see it gets us very far' — a mistake, that 'us', signalling to Hugo that he had me fairly and squarely in train. 'There must be thousands of the fellows in as many seaside resorts. It could even be abroad.'

'Oh it is very definitely in Britain,' answered Hugo. 'Notice the cyclist on the left-hand side of the road.'

Of course I hadn't, and very much wished I had, or at any rate had held my tongue.

'There's another interesting point about the road,' continued Hugo. 'Look at it closely.'

I complied.

'It seems to have metal bands down the centre,' I said at length. 'Of course; they're tram lines.'

'Exactly! There are not so many towns with trams these days. It's a pity there isn't one in the picture, as that would tell us immediately where it was taken, but of the tram-boasting resorts I've visited at one time or another, I'd be willing to bet the one in the picture is Blackpool. Great-Aunt Emily often took me there as a boy when I was staying with her in Barrow.'

I was silent for a while, studying the photograph in the vain hope of culling from it some significant detail that might have escaped Hugo.

'Even so,' I remarked at length. 'Does it really get us much further forward? Donald may well have visited Blackpool but that doesn't help us identify him or where he lives.'

'I disagree. If I'm right in believing that this was taken in Blackpool, then a visit to that jewel of a resort should enable us to locate the photographer — there can't be many, even in Blackpool. Since Donald obviously bought one of the prints, it's quite likely the photographer will have a note of his name and address.'

Inwardly I groaned. I had more than enough to keep me occupied at present and if I were to sneak off for a day or two, Blackpool would certainly not be my chosen destination. Yet the lure of an investigation finally proved irresistible. I agreed to accompany Hugo to Lancashire.

I spent the rest of the day finishing urgent jobs and Hugo picked me up at the College gate at six. He bulldozed a north-westerly course across a largish swathe of London to put us on course for my Chiltern sanctuary, which we reached about half past seven.

Since the death of my wife I had entertained few people at home, but Hugo had assembled a fair selection of provender while I had been working and we soon had a most enjoyable meal before us. We spent the evening listening to a recently purchased recording of Phillip Glass's Satyagraha which had made a great impression on me. Hugo, of course, actually understood the whole thing, Sanskrit being only one of the many languages in which he is fluent. He has long maintained that since language is the all-pervading basis of any culture, no anthropologist could seriously claim to understand a people whose tongue he could not speak. Since Hugo's interests have ranged over a great many cultures he has, in line with this doctrine, learned a multitude of languages.

When I came down the next morning Hugo was already breakfasting on the terrace. He invited me to help myself to my own provisions and enjoy the sunshine.

It was still quite early when we set off in Hugo's Rover. He struck across country to the A5, which took us in a wide sweep through the heart of Milton Keynes and then rejoining the course of Roman Watling Street we reached Towcester for an early cup of coffee in the Pickwick Café. Eventually, Hugo succumbed to the blandishments of the M1's advertising and reached even greater speeds. Bearing west on the M6 we passed through a sunny Birmingham and on to Junction 32 where we turned on to the M55.

'There's no accomplishment in driving from one corner of England to another any more,' sighed Hugo, 'no thrill of navigation; you just follow the blue signs.'

But ignore the speed limits, was my unspoken comment.

When we reached Blackpool, Hugo found a parking space with his usual mixture of good luck and secret knowledge and we walked down to the promenade. Hugo led the way to a fish and chip shop with a good view of the front.

'My aunt used to bring me here thirty years ago,' he remarked. 'It's very reassuring that it seems hardly to have changed.'

The meal was excellent of its kind and Hugo thought his aunt would still have found it acceptable. After a cup of milky tea we strolled along the promenade for half an hour or so without catching so much as a glimpse of a seaside photographer.

'I've given up a whole day to this mad

escapade for reasons which I can no longer understand,' I grumbled, 'but if there is no sign of our quarry by five, I'm catching the next train back to London. You can wander up and down the front for days on end if you like but I've got better things to do.'

Hugo merely smiled.

Late in the afternoon we were still sauntering along, and I was beginning to ache from our unnaturally slow gait and was feeling increasingly irritable. Then when even Hugo must, I'm sure, have begun to harbour doubts, we saw him.

He ambled towards us, a tall man in late middle age, with a professional looking camera hanging round his neck. While still some way off we saw him accost a couple and, with seeming ease, persuade them to pose, backs to the sea. Hugo watched closely without appearing to do so.

'Good,' he grunted. 'I was afraid he might have become a polaroid merchant but he seems to have resisted the trend.'

As the man came closer, Hugo indulged in a pantomime of gesture, pointing him out, pretending to consult me, and generally signalling his interest in the possibility of being photographed. This ploy was successful and on reaching us, the man suggested he should take a shot of Hugo. The latter struck a dramatic pose, staring out to sea, his hand shading his eyes.

'Excellent,' commented the photographer. 'I think you'll be very pleased with the result. Will you call round for it or have it sent?'

'When will it be ready?' asked Hugo.

'Tomorrow morning.'

'I'll call for it.'

'Fine. Here is my card.'

When the man had moved on, I turned to Hugo in exasperation.

'I hope you don't expect me to hole up in this place until tomorrow,' I exclaimed.

'Have you no sense of curiosity?' he enquired mildly. He handed me the photographer's business card, on which was engraved the name David Freeman. I gave it no more than a cursory glance.

'My curiosity is directed towards the study of chemistry,' I remonstrated, 'and

that entails more or less unremitting application. You may be able to justify these
jaunts by claiming they have some vague
connection with social anthropology,
but I think even you would have difficulty
in extending that claim to encompass a
genuine science.'

'Ouch!' exclaimed Hugo.

We walked on in a silence that was
somewhat less than companionable.

'I think I will at any rate just take a look
at the gentleman's abode,' Hugo remarked
after a while. 'I should be grateful if you
would come. Two pairs of trained eyes are
a great deal better than one. And there's
plenty of time before the first reasonable
train back to London.'

I grunted ungraciously, In no way
mollified by his too obvious flattery,
within which I fancied I glimpsed a strand
of irony, nevertheless I accompanied him
through a tangle of streets which Hugo
evidently recalled from childhood and we
eventually found ourselves by a corner
shop above whose entrance was the name
Freeman Fotografic. Behind the glass door
hung a 'Closed' sign and in the window

were portraits of the various stages of life from chubby babies to old age pensioners, with pride of place going to a robust looking girl in graduation robes. Hugo inspected these exhibits with seeming interest. Abruptly he took from his pocket a small case, opened it, and extracted what appeared to be a pair of opera glasses. He replaced the case and raised the glasses to his eyes. As he adjusted the focus, he remarked:

'A useful little invention this. I had an optical instrument maker fit special lenses into an old pair of opera glasses to provide strong magnification over a limited range. Ah! Very interesting. Here, look.'

He handed me the glasses and directed my scrutiny to a photograph just visible through a gap in the display at the back of the shop window. Adjusting the focus to suit my own eyesight, I saw the reason for Hugo's exclamation. The photograph was identical to that of Donald given him by Miss Spence.

As I returned the instrument to Hugo, a man came round the corner into the street. It was the photographer. He hesitated momentarily as he saw us but then came on purposefully, taking from his pocket a key as he neared the shop.

'Good afternoon gentlemen,' he said. 'I fear you are too soon to collect your photograph.'

'Of course,' replied Hugo, 'but as we were passing I thought I would ask you if you remembered a friend of mine who had his picture taken by you some while ago.'

Hugo exhibited the print he had borrowed from Miss Spence. Whether he anticipated the effect this would have I don't know but it certainly startled me. The photographer went white and although his mouth opened, no sound emerged. Hugo watched impassively. At length Freeman regained his power of speech. Peering closely at the print he answered in a voice singularly lacking in conviction.

'No . . . no, I've never seen him before.' As though realising that his countenance belied his denial, he elaborated. 'It's the light; when I first saw it I thought it was someone I knew. Now I see it isn't. The person I thought it might be . . . he died in unfortunate circumstances. That's why

I was momentarily unnerved.' Warming to this explanation, his voice and manner had become more confident.

'We have reason to believe that my friend suffered a similar fate,' answered Hugo sternly.

'But . . . that's nothing to do with me.' Freeman was obviously badly rattled again but he rallied.

'Just who are you anyway?' he demanded.

'I am Dr. Lacklan, and this is my colleague Dr. Dunkley.'

'Doctors? But . . . I don't understand. What has happened to this man, and why come to me? I told you, I've never seen him before.'

'Then how is it you have his photograph — a photograph identical to this one — on display in your shop?' countered Hugo in a voice whose quiet menace demonstrated a dramatic talent I had not known he possessed.

'What right have you . . . ?' began Freeman, his voice rising with anger, but then he stopped suddenly. From the corner of my eye I too had noticed a curtain twitch in a nearby window and now I became aware of faces at a number of other windows and of a little group of people at the end of the street observing us with interest.

'You'd better come inside,' muttered Freeman as he unlatched the shop door. He led us through the tiny shop itself into a room beyond that was little larger and, like the shop, was crowded with photographs. He switched on the light to dispel the gloom.

'Now, what the hell is this all about? Just who do you think you are, asking all these questions?'

'We have been commissioned by Miss Ophelia Spence to enquire into the sudden termination of a correspondence' answered Hugo, 'and I have every reason to believe that you can assist us, Mr. David Freeman; or should I call you Miss Deirdre Forsyth; or Box Number 7213 or even . . . Donald?'

Freeman sat down abruptly. He opened his mouth but seemed to have difficulty articulating. At length he said simply and with complete lack of originality:

'How did you find out?'

Hugo sat opposite the photographer and I followed suit. Hugo spoke now in a more normal voice.

'There were a number of indications but the final clue was the signed photograph of Miss Ophelia Spence on your mantelpiece. When I saw that everything fell into place — the simplest explanation for you having the photo-graph which Donald had admired so fulsomely, was that you were Donald. Yet you are not the man in the photograph sent to Miss Spence. You must have used a picture unwanted by its subject. Why should you do that? Your letters seemed sincere; either they were, or you have some considerable talent as a literary dissembler. That thought reminded me of Deirdre Forsyth, author of a cornucopia of popular women's fiction and I was struck, as perhaps I ought to have been before, by her initials being the same as yours and of course both of you having first names beginning with D for Donald. How neatly your various occupations fit together! Your pen-friends bureau pro-vides you with a ready-made collection of characters for your stories; your photography business with portraits to go with the persona you adopt in your correspondence with the ladies who apply to you. In a way I admire you; not only for your ingenuity, but because I imagine your deception must have brought a great deal of innocent pleasure to many lonely women and it cannot have been easy work, corresponding with so many. Nevertheless, a deception it is and for at least one of your clients, Miss Spence, it has led to some distress.'

There was silence for a while, broken eventually by Freeman.

'Your assumptions are correct as far as they go,' he answered, 'but I do not think I have behaved so badly as the bare facts might suggest. Certainly I have done nothing criminal nor illegal. I have not profited in any illicit way. The ladies who reply to my advertisements seek a quasi-anonymous pen-friend. I have been that to them. I did not set out to do so; but almost all of them are looking for the sort of man who really doesn't exist. As a writer, I am able to invent exactly what they want and all of them seem content with my efforts, all except Ophelia that is. I am well paid for my fiction, it is true, but again it satisfies a need. As far as I can see no one has been harmed by it; no one has recognised themselves, nor should they, as I've not portrayed any real individuals, merely borrowed background here and there.'

He paused as though for thought.

'Yet I must confess I feel very bad about Miss Spence.'

'You grew fond of her,' Hugo stated rather than asked.

Freeman looked up sharply.

'Why do you . . . ? Ah! of course. Hers is the only non-professional photograph I have on display. Yes, I did . . . do . . . feel a certain regard for her.' He stood up. 'Well, what do you propose to do? You can hardly have me arrested, for in the eyes of the law I've done nothing wrong. I suppose you might suggest fraud of a kind in connection with the pen-friends bureau but I doubt if you could sustain such a charge. I take it you will inform Miss Spence that she has been duped? I can assure you that that in itself would be a severe punishment, as I admit I have grown to value her good opinion.'

Hugo considered.

'I believe you,' he said finally and simply. 'And I'm sure you'll understand that Miss Spence ought to be reassured. But there's no need for me to do it rather than you.'

Freeman looked at him.

'What exactly do you mean?'

'I'll give you a week to set Miss Spence's mind at rest on the subject of Donald. If you are unable to do so then I shall feel I must do it myself.'

'Thank you,' replied Freeman, not effusively but sincerely as befitted his rather old-fashioned manner.

We left then and returned to London without more ado.

It was perhaps two weeks later that Hugo rang me to let me know the outcome of his ultimatum to Freeman.

'He played it like the hero of one of his own tales,' he announced. 'Went in person to Miss Spence, confessed everything and asked her pardon. Needless to say she was profoundly moved — what woman of her upbringing could not have been? More surprisingly, perhaps, she saw the funny side of it all; a woman with such a sense of humour must, I think, be rare. So she forgave him. Oh, and she sends us her thanks — Freeman having related our part in the affair.'

Some months later, I received an invitation: Mr. David Freeman and Miss Ophelia Spence requesting the pleasure of my company at a small celebration to follow their marriage at the Oxford Registry Office.

Naturally Hugo also was invited and at the reception I suggested that following his success in smoothing the path of true love for both Stephen and Carol, and David and Ophelia, he might well consider augmenting his income by opening a marriage bureau.

'Observe,' he replied, 'the difficulties which David Freeman encountered in running a mere pen-friends bureau and his ultimate fate. I am not tempted to take on a task even more testing.'

'I was not suggesting that you marry all

the applicants,' I smiled.

Hugo's reply was, I regret to say, typical of the man.

'How else would it be possible to find applicants the perfect husband?'

The Indian Ladder Trick

I was returning south from a visit to the remote village of Kirknewton, which nestles beneath the steep hillside of Yeavering Bell on the northern flanks of the Cheviots. On the summit of that fell is an Iron Age fortress of the ancient Britons, while in the valley had stood a sixth century palace of the Northumbrian kings. Bede recorded that here in AD 627, the missionary Paulinus converted the Northumbrians.

However, I had not been to Kirknewton to honour those dead long ago, but on a personal pilgrimage to visit the grave of my wife, buried in the tiny churchyard but five summers ago. So I was in a melancholy mood as I drove round the Newcastle bypass, and my depression was deepened by the rain that began to fall as I crossed the Tyne. The rain worsened rapidly and I was about to relieve the strain of motorway driving under such conditions by stopping for coffee at the Washington Services, when I had a sudden impulse to look up Hugo Lacklan instead.

I continued southward to the turn-off, then drove several miles along a heavily-wooded vale until I reached the mediaeval fortress in which Hugo's College houses about a third of its under-graduates and a similar proportion of its staff. I parked in the empty courtyard and made a dash for the massive wooden door which filled the castle gate-way. I unlatched the postern and stepped through into the comparative shelter of the gatehouse. Despite the gloom, the gatekeeper recognised me and gave a wave.

'If it's Dr. Lacklan you're seeking, he's in, but he has a visitor,' he remarked.

I hesitated, but only momentarily. I felt more in need of coffee and warmth than ever, so I jogged across the inner courtyard to the tower wherein Hugo has his rooms. It is one of the corner bastions of the four-square castle and rises somewhat above the massive linking walls against which the great hall and other rooms and apartments are built.

I climbed carefully the gloomy spiral stairway, with its deep worn steps, until I reached the oak door at the top of the tower. I heard Hugo's clear 'Come in' in response to my rap and I pushed open the door.

Within, all was as comfortable as one could wish. A fire blazed in the grate, survivor of many a battle between Hugo and the College Bursar. The delicious aroma of coffee emanated from a pot set on a low table between the two winged chairs flanking the fire. As I entered, Hugo and his companion rose. Hugo smiled delightedly — he has the knack of making a visitor feel the one person in the world he most wanted to welcome at that very moment!

'Come in, Alex. How splendid of you to call.'

'If it's inconvenient, just say,' I answered, more diffidently. 'I only looked in on the off-chance.'

'I'm glad you did. Please allow me to introduce you to Mrs. Desai, secretary of the Department of Anthropology.'

I turned to the woman standing quietly by the other chair. She gave a determined smile and held out a slim brown hand. She was dressed in a traditional sari and her dark hair was drawn back tightly from a face that I imagined was normally serene but now showed signs of strain.

'Dr. Dunkley is an old friend of mine,' Hugo reassured her. 'He is the ideal person to help us in the present difficulty if he can spare the time.'

All I really wanted was a cup of coffee and a warm by the fire, but it would have been discourteous to say so. Hugo, ever the perfect host, pulled up another easy chair and brought a third cup, evidently divining my inner yearning. We were soon all three seated before the burning coals and as warmth and caffeine worked upon me I began to feel better — and ready to agree to anything Hugo might suggest, just as long as I could remain comfortably ensconced in his room.

'I'm glad your views on heating still prevail over those of the Bursar,' I remarked. Hugo chuckled.

'Our last confrontation was frigidly

polite, ill-befitting the subject of our discussion,' he replied. 'He insists that central heating is more economical and I that fire is more civilised. Civilisation began with fire and when the last one dies away, civilisation will end. Consider the three of us here. Could we be any more comfortable sitting staring at a lifeless radiator? Would it encourage us to talk; to listen; to trust one another? Never! If statesmen would only meet in front of a fire, instead of a television camera, much better results might be expected from their deliberations.

'Enough of the courtesies, however,' he went on, some-what unexpectedly, 'highly though I value them. Mrs. Desai has a pressing problem and I have agreed to consider it, although promising nothing. My reputation for detection is quite unmerited and for that you must take some blame, Alex, so it'll be fitting if you can assist now.'

While I drank more coffee, Hugo explained the predicament of Mrs. Desai. Put baldly, her husband had disappeared, a commonplace enough event and hardly likely to intrigue Hugo, even though the woman was a colleague. Naturally, Mrs. Desai said she had no idea why her husband should disappear; nor did she know of anyone who would wish him harm. Of course, Hugo had advised her to inform the police, but she was reluctant to do that. She was not yet seriously worried for his safety and was intensely concerned for preserving face. So she had appealed to Hugo. He had listened at first merely with sympathy but latterly with increasing interest.

Mr. Desai had been spending all his spare time for the last few weeks repairing the roof of their house. This roof was a curious shape, the house having been originally L-shaped with intersecting gable roofs on the two arms. The angle between them had then been filled by a flat-roofed two-storey extension. When Desai was on the roof, he was not visible from the ground. Furthermore, to reach the ridge of the front gable, he really needed another ladder to set on the flat portion and not liking to borrow one, he was in the habit of hauling his own up after him on to the roof to use to reach the ridge.

A few days previously, he had been on the roof as usual and had pulled up the ladder after him. Mrs. Desai was expecting him to come down for their midday meal at one o'clock and was somewhat vexed when he did not appear on time. After a while, she went into the back yard and called to him. There was no response. She became alarmed and in time a neighbour who had heard her calls, volunteered to fetch a ladder and climb up to see what the matter was.

When he did so, he was surprised to find no sign of Mr. Desai. He and his wife helped Mrs. Desai search all round the house in case her husband had fallen but there was no trace of him. He seemed to have climbed up his ladder and vanished.

'Intriguing, isn't it?' murmured Hugo. He sat for a while immersed in his thoughts, which suited me, as I was comfortable and happy to let my mind freewheel. Our host rose abruptly, however, and crossed over to the window. The walls of the tower were three feet thick and, to reach the glazed arrow slit which served as fenestration, Hugo had to lean across a broad wedge-shaped sill.

'The rain has eased, I believe,' he remarked. 'Let us, with your permission, Mrs. Desai, go and inspect the scene. I find it a little difficult to visualise as yet.'

Reluctantly, I heaved myself from my chair and we left that warm haven for the cold stone stairs and corridors of the ancient pile. We went in Hugo's Rover, which had the merit of warmth to set against the hazard of Hugo's driving. Obviously believing the maxim that it is better to travel hopefully than to arrive, he was often so unreasonably hopeful that I for one was quite surprised to arrive at all. We rocketed down the long drive from the castle and burst upon the main road, where the hill increased our velocity. Hugo negotiated the roundabout at the bottom with all the circumspection of a charging rhinoceros, and then we were in the High Street, where traffic mercifully enforced a reduction in speed.

Shortly, however, Hugo turned left, away from the shops and into a housing estate of pre-war vintage, where privet and laurel hedges afforded concealment to all but the upper storeys of rows of mostly semi-detached houses. Mrs. Desai issued directions until we drew up outside a quite large detached house with a modicum of front garden. We all got out. The rain was still in abeyance, but the air felt chill and damp and smelt of rank vegetation. The house was more or less as Hugo had described it to me. Mrs. Desai led us round the side of the building, through a latched wooden gate to the back. The neighbour's ladder still leaned against the wall of the house where the flat roof was.

'Steady the ladder, there's a good chap,' requested Hugo.

He went up rapidly and held the top while I climbed after him. From the flat roof of the extension, there was a good view behind the house and to one side, but in the other directions the roof rose steeply. Hugo was standing deep in thought.

Mr. Desai's ladder was in two parts. What was clearly the upper half scaled the gable close by one of the stacks. The other lay across the flat roof with about a third of it protruding over the edge. A large bucket lay on its side close by. I shook my head.

'What on earth can have happened to the fellow?' I asked Hugo, 'If he'd jumped, he must have left some mark on landing, even if he was lucky enough not to break a leg. Perhaps he was lifted off by helicopter! Or maybe he just climbed up his ladder and disappeared when he got to the top — a sort of Indian ladder trick!'

He gave no sign of amusement at this, merely answering impatiently.

'Oh, that's no problem. It's quite obvious how he left the roof. The interesting questions are why — and where he is now.'

I was piqued.

'It may be obvious to you, but I can't see it,' I returned rather stiffly.

'Surely it's quite clear?' he chided. 'You're a scientist, trained to observe and to make deductions. Note the position of the ladder, the bucket, and this painter's hook. Then observe over there that flat-roofed shed in the adjoining garden, with the broom leaning against it. Well? Is all now revealed?'

I had to admit it was not.

'But surely,' began Hugo, then perhaps remembering how much more percipient he is than mere ordinary mortals, he started again in the sort of kindly tone one might use to an earnest but dull undergraduate.

'Imagine, if you will, Mr. Desai here on the roof. He wishes to depart in such a way that it will appear he is still up here, thus presumably allowing him a head start in case anyone tries to follow him.

'Normally, he climbs up to the roof using the two sections fitted together, pulls them up after him, and separates the top half to use in reaching the ridge. When he's ready to descend, he puts the ladder back together and lowers it over the side.

'Yesterday, however, he used just the lower section, grounding it on the roof of that shed. The ladder was then a bit short of its target and, instead of overlapping the roof edge, it rested against the wall about a metre down. I noticed two marks on the stucco about the right distance apart and below the gutter.

'He then carried the upper section with him, until he could manoeuvre it on to the roof, whereupon, by standing on the top rung of the bottom section, he could get enough purchase to haul himself up on to the roof. He next set the upper section on the slope of the roof, where you now see it, and descended to the shed roof, the way he came up. He would have had an anxious moment dangling over the edge until his feet connected with the ladder, I don't doubt.

'After that, however, everything was reasonably easy. He took down the ladder, attached that bucket full of water to the top rung with the painter's hook and then manoeuvred the ladder back up the wall. Getting it over the edge of the roof without dislodging the bucket must have been tricky, but he probably turned it sideways on.

'With his arms extended or, more likely, using that broom as a pusher, he must have slid the ladder up far enough for the weight of the bucket to swing it down and at that moment he would have pushed hard to ensure that the ladder was carried forward, so that when the bucket overturned and the water spilled out, it nevertheless did not swing back.'

I stared at Hugo. Once explained, of course, it was straightforward enough, but I doubted whether I would ever have worked it out myself. My self-doubt must have shown on my face as Hugo suddenly grinned.

'Now you know how your students feel when you show them just how to calculate the pH of a solution containing a weak acid and its salt. All is confusion! The master speaks, and lo — all is revealed as simplicity itself!'

I grunted. I didn't care for the analogy and I didn't care for Hugo knowing more about chemistry than I do about anthropology. However, Hugo was once again worrying over the problem of why Desai had done a bunk.

'Perhaps he saw something that interested him,' I remarked lightly. Hugo stared.

'Of course! One up to you, old man!'

I smiled, I hoped insouciantly, not having intended my observation seriously. Hugo, however, was not looking at me but was scanning the surrounding scene intently. He evidently failed to find anything of interest for he soon turned his attention to the section of ladder against the sloping roof.

'Here, hold this fast,' he ordered. I obeyed and up he went. Within a few minutes, he returned, a triumphant expression on his face.

'Well done! You've hit the nail on the head! Up you go and have a look.'

I did so, with some trepidation, feeling very exposed to the cold wind. Nervously, I clutched the chimney stack at the apex of the roof and half-heartedly surveyed the surroundings — neat rectangular gardens with lawns, trees and shrubs. Enlightenment failed to come. I descended and told Hugo so; he seemed disappointed, but didn't offer to remedy my deficiencies as a sleuth.

'Come on,' he said instead. 'I'm pretty sure of the facts now, but we might as well check.' We went back to ground level.

'Was your husband quite a tall man, Mrs. Desai?' Hugo asked.

'About your height,' she asserted. Hugo nodded with satisfaction, obviously feeling this confirmed his explanation of the ladder trick.

'Was he by any chance originally from Agra?'

'Yes,' she answered in surprise.

'Good!' exclaimed Hugo. 'I believe I now understand why your husband has run away and I feel sure he will return. However, before explaining it to you I should like to check one further point. Please be patient for a short while longer.'

We left a puzzled Mrs. Desai at her front gate. Hugo led me to the corner of the deserted street and round into the next.

'I think the eleventh house is the one,' he murmured. We reached it, he unlatched the gate and we strode up to the door. An elderly man answered our knock.

'I'm sorry to trouble you,' began Hugo in his most courteous manner, 'but I should very much like to ask a question about your garden.'

The man's eyebrows rose.

'You've spent time in India?' asked Hugo.

'Yes,' was the curt response. 'Diplomatic corps. Do I know you, sir?'

Hugo smiled engagingly.

'No, indeed. I'm looking into the disappearance of a gentleman who lives round the corner, in Harthope Drive. From his roof he can see your garden. I believe it was that which precipitated his departure. He was originally from Agra, you see.'

The man's demeanour changed perceptibly.

'I do see; yes, it is possible. Please, come through.'

Mystified, I followed the ex-diplomat and Hugo through the neat bungalow to an equally well-tended garden behind and down a flagged path. Then at last all became clear, even to me. A rectangular brick-edged pond reflected in its still surface an image of the Taj Mahal, exquisitely modelled in miniature on the far side of the pool.

'It's beautiful,' said Hugo, 'and, unless

I'm mistaken, exact in every detail.'

'You are not mistaken,' answered the old man. 'The happiest posting of my long service was in Uttar Pradesh. Many times I visited the Taj. There is nothing like it anywhere in the world. This, of course, cannot do it justice but sometimes in Spring, at dawn, if I stand here and half close my eyes, I can recapture something of the effect the sight of it used to have on me.'

Hugo nodded.

'No one who has seen it can ever entirely escape it's spell,' he murmured. 'Poor Desai mending his roof, must have glimpsed it from his unaccustomed vantage point and it brought on a sudden overwhelming home-sickness. I don't doubt for a moment that he has gone to see it again, perhaps for the last time in his life. He wanted to go at once and alone, hence his dramatic departure. He'll return, I'm sure; his life now is here.'

We returned to the Desais' house, where we found Mrs. Desai holding a postcard. She handed it to Hugo without a word and we both read it.

It was from Desai. He wrote simply, if a bit incoherently, to the effect that he was sorry to rush off, he couldn't really explain, but she was not to worry, he'd be back and he'd write again soon. Hugo told the woman what he believed to be the reason behind her husband's abrupt departure. To my relief, she seemed to accept it calmly enough.

'I take it his passport has gone?' Hugo asked.

She went to see and on returning confirmed that it had and also a very small case and a few clothes.

'Not enough,' she sighed.

'You ought really to inform the police,' Hugo suggested gently, 'for his and your protection in case I am wrong and something has happened to him.'

She shook her head vigorously.

'I have faith in your judgement,' she answered simply. And so we left her and returned to the castle. I accepted Hugo's invitation to stay for lunch and then resumed my journey south.

A month later, I encountered Hugo on one of his frequent visits to London and enquired if there had been any further developments in the matter of the Desais.

'She had another postcard from him, from Agra,' smiled Hugo. 'He wrote that she should expect him back on the first of September. The picture on the card was the Taj Mahal by moonlight.'

Opus Posthumous

Hugo Lacklan and I sat in the gloom of the drawing room of Five Trees. Our armchairs faced the French windows and I could see dim shapes of shrubs crouching in the darkling garden and the upright sentries of poplars further away, framing a sweep of the Malverns thrusting high above the Severn plain, black against a sky in which the more luminous stars were already twinkling. Into the silence which had fallen with the setting of the sun, came the sound of the piano in the room above, played by Charles Salgo's amanuensis, Peter Maitland.

We listened for a while, Hugo sitting entranced, myself struggling to perceive the music hidden in the notes. Difficult though I found Salgo's music, there were some pieces that I had learnt to enjoy and I strove to build on that appreciation; to follow the musical thoughts of Charles Salgo, new thoughts that none but ourselves had yet heard. To be within earshot of a living composer at work on his latest composition was a privilege accorded to few and even to my poorly-tutored ear the sound of great music struggling to be born was evident. The composer was clearly concentrating on a few phrases, forming them, like a sculptor, by chipping away all that was unnecessary, to reach the absolute essentials inherent in his ideas. I found it a moving experience, an affirmation of the essential immortality of the works of man, of his fitness to inhabit the marvel of the cosmos, however far and however often he sank into the mires of bestiality.

The events leading to our presence in that room had begun at a concert in the Barbican, a concert of English music in which a new composition by Salgo was the climax to a feast of works by Elgar, Vaughan Williams, Delius and Havergal Brian. It was the third in a series of such galas perhaps intended to demonstrate the continuity of modern English composition, despite the diversity of styles. In the previous concerts, we had been treated to orchestral music by Parry and Stanford, Britten and Bax, Holst and Bridge, Finzi and Moeran, Ireland and Arnold, Bliss and Warlock. All of it was orchestral music, for the compositions of Charles Salgo were entirely for that medium. Unusually for an Englishman, he had written nothing for voice, neither solo nor choral works, and the object of the series was to establish Salgo once and for all as the latest in the line of English musical genius.

After the rigmarole of clapping the conductor on and off the stage was over, we left the auditorium, secured glasses of beer from the café, and sat in the warm evening watching the fountains play. Hugo remained for some time lost in whatever inner visions the music had evoked for him. Eventually however he spoke — Hugo is never silent for long!

'Well, what did you think of Salgo's latest?'

'I found it hard listening,' I admitted, 'but there are things in it I could appreciate immediately, and I'm sure with repeated hearing I can learn to enjoy it as

I have some of his other works.'

'Yet it is a curious piece,' he mused. 'In places, it seemed as though he were striking out into new territory, in others as though he were returning to places already thoroughly explored.'

'And why shouldn't he?' I demanded. 'It seems in some ways sensible to mix the new with the familiar, if that makes the work more accessible to the listener.'

'Modern composers are rarely sensible, and hardly ever concerned with making life easy for their audience,' replied Hugo sardonically. 'Still, that isn't really what puzzles me about the work.' He hesitated. 'I think it is something more technical. If you can spare a while, I'd like to show you what I mean, to see if you agree.'

I acquiesced, but with some misgivings, as Hugo is an amateur musicologist of some repute, whilst I understand next to nothing about the technicalities of the art. I know what I like and I'm prepared to put some effort into widening my horizons, but purely as a listener. We crossed the windy plaza of the Barbican to Shakespeare Tower, in which Hugo has a flat, and ascended to his eyrie. A fairly tedious hour ensued, with Hugo trying to demonstrate to me with talk of serial music and supertonics, polyphony and polyrhythms, that Salgo's development as a composer was quite unlike any other.

'Of course,' he mused. 'He's over ninety now, but there's no diminution of vigour or invention in his work; it's really no more than a mismatch of styles that puzzles me. The obvious explanation is that, because he has to dictate his compositions to an amanuensis, the latter is influencing what he writes — but is that really credible? To become a successful composer calls for a degree of artistic integrity which is scarcely in accord with such an idea.'

'Could it not be a genuine collaboration?' I suggested. Hugo was sceptical but agreed there was no evidence against such an idea.

'However, I don't believe it. This remains a fascinating conundrum. I've been making a study of the relationship between Delius and Eric Fenby, and there I see no sign that the composer was influenced by Fenby. Anyway, I'm writing an article on the phenomenon, so I've been in contact with Maitland, and Salgo's very kindly invited me to visit his home, Five Trees. Maitland says that Salgo will not see anyone, but Maitland himself is willing to be interviewed.' Hugo smiled. 'I may have over-emphasised the importance I intend to assign to his rôle in Salgo's music.'

'I bet you did! I hope he won't be offended when he sees your article in print.' Hugo ignored this.

'I mentioned to Maitland that you too were an admirer of Salgo and he said that you would be very welcome to accompany me if you wished to do so.'

I stared at Hugo balefully.

'Why on earth did you do that? You know how ignorant I am about music. I'd be bored stiff.'

'I'm not so sure,' answered Hugo unrepentantly. 'I have a feeling that something very odd is going on at Five Trees, not just in the musical sense. I'd be grateful if you could spare the time to come.'

This, from Hugo, was distinctly flattering.

'You scent a mystery,' I remarked. 'One of your enigmas, in fact, and you want me to come and admire you solving it.'

Hugo demurred.

'If there is anything to be discovered, the chances of doing so will be more than doubled if there are two of us to poke about.'

In the end I acquiesced, more because I love the Malverns than for any other reason.

We motored down in my car. Five Trees was on the outskirts of Great Malvern, and the garden was dominated by five immense trees, around which had grown up so many others that the house was practically hidden by a small wood. I drove carefully along the grand drive and drew up by a flight of steps leading to a gloomy Victorian house. We were met at the front door by Maitland and his wife, who both seemed a little wary in their greetings.

'It's most unlikely that Charles himself will be able to see you,' was almost the first thing Peter Maitland said. 'He seldom sees anyone now.' Hugo was reassuring.

'It is really you I would like to talk to,' he said. 'For the purpose of my article.'

Maitland looked pleased. He was a tall, stooped, short-sighted man in his early forties.

'I get the feeling from studying Salgo's output over the last ten years or so,' Hugo went on, 'that you may be something more than an amanuensis,' Hugo went on, 'more perhaps of a collaborator?'

'It's all Charles' music,' Maitland answered somewhat abruptly. 'All I do is write it down at his dictation. Sometimes I fill in a bit of orchestration, but only at his behest.' Hugo nodded and did not pursue the subject, but I supposed that it was a matter to which he would return.

Mrs. Maitland showed us to our rooms. She was shorter than her husband but slim, with a pleasant rather than beautiful face. The house was large and divided in two by the large entrance hall from which an imposing staircase rose to a gallery. Cynthia Maitland directed us to the right.

She explained that Salgo's rooms were to the left, and that she and her husband had their bedroom next to the composer's, in case he should need anything at any time of the night.

My own room was at the back of the house and overlooked a garden, which seemed to have reverted almost to a wilderness. Young beech trees and sycamores were growing in rough grass, which I guessed had once been a lawn, and the boundaries were completely obscured by a tangle of mature trees and young bushes, and perhaps the spreading of hedges left unchecked. Hugo's room was next to mine and had one window looking out to the front, where the lawn was at any rate roughly cut, and the hedge showed signs of having been chopped back in the not too distant past, affording glimpses of the high ridge of the Malverns to the west.

Mrs. Maitland had set a supper for four in a large dining room which would have been thoroughly cheerless had it not been for a huge fire burning in the grate.

'We've plenty of logs from the garden,' remarked Maitland. 'The autumn gales

143

always bring a tree or two down.'

Both he and his wife seemed more relaxed as we chatted about neutral topics.

'Were you at the recent première of The Malvern Suite?' asked Hugo during a lull in the conversation.

Maitland nodded.

'I went up to London for it. Unfortunately, we couldn't both go as one of us must stay to look after Charles, but I'm hoping it will be recorded soon. Lyrita are interested in bringing it out. Then Cynthia will be able to hear it as it should sound.' He smiled. 'We lived with it day and night during its composition, and Cynthia often played bits of it through on the piano so that Charles could experience it.'

'I imagine Mr. Salgo will be anxious to hear a recording of the orchestral version himself,' observed Hugo.

'Hm? Oh, yes, yes of course.' Maitland seemed to lose interest and began talking of something else.

After supper, the Maitlands excused themselves, on the grounds that they normally spent the evening with Salgo.

'I've put a pot of coffee and a decanter of port in the drawing-room,' said Cynthia Maitland. 'I hope you'll be comfortable in there.'

Hugo and I thanked her for the excellent repast and as the Maitlands climbed the stair we crossed the hallway to the drawing-room where too, there was a log fire blazing. By unspoken consent, we took chairs facing the west window to watch the sun set behind the high hills. As its light dimmed, that of the dancing flames became more insistent and at length we turned our chairs to face the fire's welcome warmth. How long the composer and his pianist toiled, I don't know, for the music still filtered down when Hugo rose at eleven, to say he thought an early night would do him good. As the decanter was empty and the fire burning lower, there seemed indeed no reason to linger.

The walls of the old house were thick and no music penetrated from the other side of the gallery. In fact, it was so quiet that I had some difficulty in falling asleep.

* ★ ★ ★

Both Hugo and I are early risers, and the next morning we met in the dining-room at 7.30, to find the table already laden with breakfast. I usually have no more than a bowl of cereal, but the offer of bacon, egg, toast and marmalade was not to be refused. The Maitlands did not join us, Mrs. Maitland having placed the cooked food in hot dishes on a sideboard.

'I think a brisk walk is in order after that,' remarked Hugo, as he poured himself a final cup of coffee. In the event, our outing was anything but brisk. We toiled slowly up a steep and zigzagging street which climbed the precipitous flank of the Malvern ridge. Houses clung to the rock, or nestled in grottos gouged out of the scarp. The sky was cloudless and the sun made climbing hot work, so I was glad when we had left the houses behind and reached the crest of the ridge. We lodged ourselves on a seat conveniently placed to view the landscape spread out below us. The Malverns rise so abruptly from the plain that they give an exaggerated impression of their height. Far to the east, other hills rose into the haze, but directly below us was the edge of Great Malvern.

'There's Five Trees.' Hugo pointed it out as though I couldn't see it for myself. He'd brought with him a pair of powerful binoculars and through these he proceeded to study the home of Charles Salgo. After a while he passed them to me.

'What do you make of that area on the south side of the house?'

'It seems to be a walled garden,' I answered after perusing it for a while. 'Very overgrown. There's a small stone out-house in one corner.'

'Notice anything else?'

'No, I can't see anything else.'

'Exactly!' remarked Hugo triumphantly.

'What do you mean?'

'What, in particular, you don't see and neither do I, is any gate or doorway through the walls. The garden is entirely enclosed by three unbroken walls cutting it off from the rest of the garden, and by the side of the house. Which suggests?'

'That there must be a door opening into it from the house itself. Perhaps if we walked further along the ridge to the south we'd be able to see it.'

The narrow Malvern ridge rises and falls steeply but not greatly, and following it from one summit to the next is an easy task. Our distance from Five Trees meant that we had to walk some considerable way before we subtended a sufficient angle to view the wall of the house fronting the garden.

Hugo raised his glasses and scanned the building. Then, without a word, he passed the binoculars to me. A wooden door opening into the garden was plain to see. Furthermore, a narrow flight of stone steps with a metal guard rail led down from another door in the upper storey.

'Interesting,' I remarked, 'but hardly enigmatic.'

'You think not?' said Hugo. 'Where then is that door? Into which room of the house does it open?'

I thought for a moment.

'It must be into the drawing room,' I began, but my conviction faltered, for

I could see in my mind's eye the interior of that room in which we had spent the previous evening, and it had only one door — the one leading to the hall. The French windows were on the other side.

'So the door has been blocked up or concealed,' I conceded. 'That I suppose is of some interest.'

I surveyed the house through the field-glasses once again, and was just in time to see Maitland emerge from the door in the upper storey and descend the steps to the garden. He traversed the length of it slowly, his head bowed, his hands clasped behind him, as though deep in thought. His progress was far from aimless, however, since it brought him directly to the stone outhouse I had noted in the angle of the walls. He went inside. Hugo and I sat on in the sunshine and waited. Some half-an-hour later, Maitland emerged and returned to the house. Hugo continued to study the building through the binoculars for a while. At length, he proffered them to me again.

'There's a cable issuing from a hole in

the house wall, some two feet up, and going down the wall to ground level. If you look at the outhouse, you will see a similar length of cable against its wall.'

I agreed this was true.

'They must have installed electric lighting in that outhouse for some reason,' I said.

'More than lighting. That's a power cable; 13 amps at least.'

'Perhaps they keep the freezer down there,' I said.

Hugo looked at me curiously.

'I wonder if you're right.'

He would say no more about what his own ideas were, and we rambled on along the ridge in silence, before returning the way we had come in time for lunch. The meal was excellently suited to my simple tastes, and the Maitlands, who had joined us, seemed a little more forthcoming than on the previous evening.

Hugo had succeeded in overcoming Maitland's reticence about his relationship with the composer, by concentrating on the very early period when Salgo was reluctantly coming to terms with the paralysis in his limbs and, unable to write any longer, he would pour out his musical invention to Peter Maitland in a mixture of singing, humming and dictated notation. I talked to Cynthia Maitland about ballet, in which she had a passionate interest, although her appreciation of it was now confined to television performances due to Salgo's need for continual attention. I'm not mad about the dance myself, but I have a fair knowledge of it, and I fancy she enjoyed our conversation.

Over coffee, Peter Maitland announced that he and his wife would be going into Worcester that afternoon.

'Charles is sleeping,' he said, 'and is unlikely to wake for several hours. It is his normal pattern. He works late into the night, and then sleeps away the day. It is sometimes hard for us but . . . ' he shrugged. 'It is a privilege to serve so great an artist.'

'Are you going out again this afternoon?' Cynthia Maitland asked.

'I rather think I might take a nap myself,' answered Hugo. 'The peace of Five Trees is beginning to relax me, and I find myself feeling quite tired — as though all the fatigue I've been putting off for months has finally caught up with me.'

'And you?' Peter Maitland directed the question at me.

'I'm staying in, too,' I replied. 'I've brought with me a review article I've nearly finished, and I'll spend the afternoon polishing it up.'

I noticed the Maitlands exchange glances but exactly what their expressions signified I couldn't decide, although I fancied I detected an underlying apprehension.

★   ★   ★

When lunch was over, Hugo went up to his bedroom. I sat in the drawing-room, where the fire was already lit, and started work on my article. Presently, I heard the front door close and then the sound of a car being started, followed by a scrunching on gravel as it headed for the road, and then silence.

Some five minutes later, the door to the

drawing-room opened and Hugo entered.

'Hello,' I said. 'Not tired after all?'

He smiled.

'Just a ruse to allay our hosts' evident disquiet at leaving us alone in the house.'

'Alone with Charles Salgo, you mean?'

'No, I meant what I said.'

I stared at him, and opened my mouth to protest at such nonsense, but my objections were still-born as I saw myself that they amounted to nothing.

Hugo nodded, obviously having followed my train of thought.

'We haven't seen Salgo, haven't heard him, have come across no sign of him whatsoever. All we have is the assertion of the Maitlands that he is upstairs. There is nothing impossible in such a state of affairs, but it doesn't seem right. Everything goes so smoothly and silently. People who knew him said Salgo was always a self-centred man and his illness made him downright cantankerous. If he is living in this house, I'm convinced that there'd be some evidence of it — if not his raised voice, then certainly some disruption of routine.'

'Then what do you believe has happened to him?'

'There are a number of possibilities,' answered Hugo, 'and I'm not yet ready to come down in favour of any particular one. We need more facts and I think we'll find them in that out-house.'

Hugo was inspecting the wall of the room as he spoke, and at length pointed to a set of built-in bookshelves.

'That is the most likely position of the concealed door,' he said. 'Although it appears to be blocked up rather than hidden.'

Removal of some of the volumes confirmed his suspicion.

'There's no way through there without a pickaxe,' he remarked. 'Which leaves the door and outside staircase from the rooms above.'

'But if Salgo is there after all . . . '

'If he is, then my suspicions are negated,' Hugo replied.

Dubiously, I followed him out of the room and up the staircase where, instead of turning right towards our own rooms, Hugo made a decisive turn to the left.

Silent on the thick carpet, he moved to the nearest door and turned the handle with no attempt at care or concealment. Doubtless, if Salgo was there and Hugo disturbed him, he would apologise and claim to have been so deep in thought that he didn't realise where he was. However the room was empty.

I waited a little anxiously, since I'd no wish for a scene, while Hugo deliberately blundered into the other rooms on the south side of the house. My relief that no disturbance ensued was offset by a mixture of annoyance at the trick that the Maitlands had played on us, and alarm at its implications.

'No Salgo,' remarked Hugo unnecessarily. 'The door to the outside staircase is in that room there. I suggest we use it to reach the garden.'

I must admit I hoped the door to the stair would be locked, but in this I was disappointed. We descended what was evidently a fire escape and so gained access to the walled garden. Hugo lost no time in making for the stone-built outhouse, and I followed him with some reluctance along a path hedged with tall thick yews, again hoping for a locked door and once more being disappointed.

We entered the windowless structure and Hugo found a switch which bathed the room in the golden glow of concealed lighting. It was empty, save for a large chest freezer. Hugo lifted the lid and we looked in.

There was no mistaking the frozen corpse of Charles Salgo. Photographs of him are rare, but his features are too distinctive for doubt. We did not look long, and I for one was glad to get out into the sunshine again.

'What are you going to do?' I asked.

Unusually, Hugo hesitated.

'It depends, I think, on the explanation.'

'But he's dead!' I expostulated. 'And the Maitlands are pretending he's still alive. What explanation can there be, than that they've concealed the fact so that they can go on living here? Unless — are you suggesting they actually murdered him?'

'No,' replied Hugo, still thoughtful.

'No, I don't see any reason to suppose that; I can't at the moment imagine a motive. But you are forgetting the music. That surely is far more interesting than confirmation of my suspicion that Salgo is dead. The music we've been hearing is, I feel, undeniably Salgo's.'

'Well then, it must be something he was working on when he died, something that hadn't been published.'

'No, no.' Hugo shook his head emphatically. 'That I don't believe! What we've heard since we arrived is new music struggling to be born, not just a pretence.'

A scrunch of tyres on gravel interrupted our discussion.

'They've returned!' I said in alarm, and started towards the house.

'Wait!' commanded Hugo, and I stopped. 'Let's stay here until they come. Our presence in the garden will save the tedium of accusation and the charade of protested ignorance.'

I was unhappy about this course of action, not because I felt there was any likelihood of danger in it, but because I detest scenes, and the prospect of Mrs.

Maitland collapsing in hysterics was disconcerting in the extreme. I did her an injustice.

We had not long to wait for the Maitlands to appear at the top of the staircase. It was as though they had expected us to be here in the forbidden garden, and indeed this turned out to be the case. They descended and came towards us. I breathed deep of the fragrance of sweet rocket that filled the bed by the path, and waited for the storm to break.

'This is an unwarranted intrusion!' declared Maitland angrily. 'Not the behaviour to be expected of guests, still less of cultured ones.'

'Hush, Peter,' Cynthia intervened. 'I'm sure they acted properly according to their lights.'

'It's an impertinence,' muttered her husband.

'I do indeed apologise for trespassing on your privacy,' answered Hugo, in a voice of evident sincerity, 'but suspecting what I did, the only real alternative was to report those suspicions to the police and that I was reluctant to do.'

This statement evidently had a salutary effect on Peter Maitland, although it was clear that his wife had been more perceptive than he, and had already appreciated that aspect of the situation.

'To be brief,' continued Hugo, 'we have seen the body of Charles Salgo. It is clearly our civic duty to go to the police and report what we have seen, but we might be persuaded that it would not be wrong to delay for a short while.'

'Yes, yes please give us a little time,' appealed Cynthia Maitland.

'You must tell us why you have perpetrated this deception.' Hugo was quietly insistent.

'Yes, of course. We must tell them, Peter,' she urged her husband.

'I suppose you are right,' he conceded grudgingly.

'Then let us return to the house,' commanded Hugo briskly, 'and have our explanations in comfort.'

The Maitlands preceded us up the iron staircase and through the rooms once occupied by the deceased composer. The woman said something in a low voice to her husband, and then turned to us.

'Let's go into the drawing-room,' she suggested. 'Peter is going to make us all some coffee. I feel it is my responsibility to tell you what happened, as it was at my insistence that we acted as we did.'

We sat in comfortable chairs round the low, tiled coffee table in the window. Cynthia Maitland thought for a moment, and when she began she did so eliptically.

'We had no intention of it going on for so long.' She paused and was silent until Hugo prompted her.

'Just how long ago was it that Charles died?'

'It was nearly six months,' she confessed.

I was astonished but Hugo seemed unsurprised.

'Charles was working on the last movement of his Malvern Suite, but as was usual with him, he had already begun to plan his next composition. He had sketched out some of the main themes and the overall scope of the work. He was dictating to Peter, of course, since he could do nothing for himself physically.

'It was a Saturday evening and Charles

worked late, which meant that Peter and I did so too, and so we were not up on the Sunday morning as early as we might have been.'

At this point, there was an interruption, as Peter Maitland brought in the coffee and we busied ourselves with pouring it. Cynthia Maitland resumed.

'When Peter took Charles' tea into him, he found that during the night, the spirit had left his body. Our first thought was that it was a merciful release. For his restless psyche to have been trapped so long in that useless body must have been purgatory. Now it was free to enter the next phase of existence. We arranged the body in a tidy way on the bed and then Peter went to telephone the doctor. Not that there was any doubt at all of death but we both understood this was the right thing to do. However, the doctor was out and Peter has always hated those answerphone machines. When asked to record a message, he always hangs up. He tried several more times during the rest of the day but without success.

'That afternoon, still tired I suppose

from the previous evening's work, I dozed off in my armchair here in this very room. When I awoke, Charles was standing close by — I swear this is the absolute truth — regarding me with that familiar air of impatience to be about his art that he had always had and seemingly free of his former infirmity.'

She smiled.

'I felt no fear at this visitation from beyond, nor did I have any doubt that that was what it was. When he saw I was awake, Charles spoke to me. He had passed on too soon, he said. His Malvern Suite must be finished. He told me to go upstairs to his room, to the piano. I did as he bid, and when I got there he was waiting for me. He could not play himself, he explained. Once the spirit has relinquished the body, it can no longer interact with matter, but if I would let him, he could play through me.'

Again Cynthia paused, reliving the experience of that first session with the dead composer. It was impossible to disbelieve her sincerity. Whatever had actually happened on that occasion, she herself was clearly convinced that she had experienced a benign possession.

'That was the beginning,' she resumed. 'When Peter heard the sound of the piano from Charles' room, he came and found me playing, as though I was in a trance. He couldn't see Charles; he never has seen him, but he doesn't doubt he's there, because of the music.'

Peter Maitland nodded. Now that their secret had been discovered, his uneasiness and uncertain temper had disappeared.

'It was music I'd never heard before,' he commented. 'Yet, beyond the slightest doubt, it was Salgo's music. As my first astonishment and alarm passed, it was succeeded by a sense of the urgency of capturing the essence of the music that my wife was playing under the spell of the greatest of living composers, regardless of the fact that he was already dead. He worked us hard that night, afraid, as he explained, that he would soon be drawn away from Five Trees for ever. Eventually, my wife fell asleep at the keyboard from sheer exhaustion.'

Cynthia smiled a tight smile, as the

memory of her labours came back to her.

'The next day I went round in a dream,' she said. 'Peter looked after me as though I was a child. Charles came again that evening, and we worked on The Malvern Suite once more.'

'I was in a quandary,' Peter took up the story again. 'Both of us were eager to see the opus finished and we both felt that, if Charles' body was removed from Five Trees, it might snap the link that allowed him to return. Not having been able to contact our doctor, we were still the only ones who knew Charles had died. He has no family, and there seemed no harm in delaying an announcement of his death if that would allow the completion of his last and perhaps greatest work. Still, we could not possibly leave his body where it was. It was then I remembered the old chest freezer we'd had installed in that outhouse in the days when Charles liked to entertain. It needed some minor repairs which I easily effected, and the evening after he died we transferred his body to it.'

'I was quite agitated about doing even

that,' resumed Cynthia, 'in case it broke the link. But my fears were unnecessary. He continued to come.'

She paused, and poured more coffee.

'Although the work on The Malvern Suite seemed to be going well, unrelated material kept intruding. At length, Charles explained that the symphony he had intended to write when The Suite was finished, was already far advanced in his subconscious, to which he now had much readier access than when he was trapped in his body. It was to be his greatest achievement; it must be written.

'How could we refuse him?' Cynthia Maitland asked. 'Once The Malvern Suite was finished, we began work in earnest on the Symphony. So you see, we didn't deliberately conceal Charles' physical demise; it had just come about and his body no longer seemed especially important. We left it safe in the freezer, until he should finally relinquish all hold on the physical world. That moment is now close at hand; the Symphony is almost finished. You won't prevent its successful completion, will you?'

So there it was; as difficult a decision as I have ever had to make, and all as a result of allowing myself to be drawn into one of Hugo's exercises in curiosity.

'You must give us a little while to think over what you have said,' Hugo temporized, but once he and I were on our own, it quickly emerged that his mind was made up. However, he had rightly foreseen that I would have grave reservations about the affair — which he now set about overcoming.

'On the one hand,' he argued, 'there is to be set the conclusion of a major musical opus, for it will be that, I have no doubt from what I have heard; on the other, conformity with a minor legal technicality. What crime have the Maitlands committed? None, I am sure. They have delayed reporting a death from natural causes: a misdemeanour, of course, and not one to be encouraged in normal circumstances. But these are not normal circumstances. You may not believe that Charles Salgo is actually composing his symphony and transmitting it from beyond the grave, but the

Maitlands clearly do.

'If you are sceptical, you may, even so, accept my assurance that what they are producing is genuine Salgo. It may come from the depths of their own subconscious, from seeds sown there by the composer during his lifetime, and growing in soil made fertile by long association with him. And what difference is there in reconstructing a work from remembered snatches and descriptions and in doing so from pieces of manuscript and recorded fragments as in the case of Elgar's third symphony? But in a sense that scarcely matters. What is important is that it is, in my opinion, a work of undoubted genius and to deny it to the world would be a truly criminal act. If we expose the Maitlands' technical infringement of the law, I suspect we would kill their creative activity stone dead as surely as if we were really severing a link with the spirit of the dead man, as the Maitlands would believe.'

There was more of the same. It didn't entirely convince me, but it left me feeling doubtful enough to be effectively paralysed. We left Five Trees soon afterwards.

All this occurred almost a year ago. About a month after our departure, it was announced that Charles Salgo, the gifted composer, had passed away peacefully in his sleep. There was no suggestion in the reports I read of anything untoward about the time or manner of his decease. I had heard from an acquaintance, who is a professor of pathology at one of the London medical schools, that 'my friend' Hugo had quizzed him about the effects of prolonged freezing of a body on determination of the passage of time since death occurred, ostensibly in connection with an anthropological investigation Hugo was carrying out into the customs of ice burial of a remote Siberian tribe. I was non-committal, but felt naturally suspicious that Hugo was, in reality, obtaining information that might assist the Maitlands to pull the wool over the eyes of Salgo's doctor, whom they would naturally have called in when the time came. The less I knew about it, the better it was for me, was my opinion.

Salgo's Posthumous Symphony, when it was finally performed, was hailed as a masterpiece. Hugo and I attended that premier at The Royal Festival Hall and afterwards dined in a small Italian restaurant not far from the concert hall. Somewhat incautiously, I asked Hugo if he was entirely happy that the symphony should be included in the canon of Salgo's works.

'Is it right to conceal what we know?' I asked.

'What do we know?'

'We know it isn't really Salgo's music,' I replied.

'Do we? The Maitlands believe it is. The critics accept that it is! I very much doubt that anyone would believe us if we were to question it.'

I was not so sure. I felt certain that a thorough forensic investigation of Salgo's corpse by a skilled pathologist might even now reveal discrepancies between the actual and supposed date of death. Hugo disposed of this with devastating ease.

'He was cremated,' he said.

'At your suggestion, perhaps?'

'I really can't remember.'

'Even so,' I persisted in making one last effort, 'you know the truth. Indeed, you deduced that something was seriously wrong with The Malvern Suite, simply on musicological grounds, before we even visited Malvern. Don't you want the credit for penetrating a musical fraud that has deceived even professional musicians?'

'No,' answered Hugo. 'I may have faults, but vanity isn't one of them.'

The audacity of this claim left me with no words for further argument.

Bequest

It was on the brief journey from Shadwell to Limehouse on the Docklands Light Railway that Hugo Lacklan told me the short and singular tale of Mr. Milton's travelling companion. He claimed it was not one of his own but a true story related to him by an elderly acquaintance who thought it would interest him. Hugo was only a boy when introduced to Mr. Milton and he had never got out of the habit of referring to him in this rather formal way.

According to Hugo, Mr. Milton commuted to London on the line into Marylebone, and travelling by the same train every morning he came to know many of his fellow passengers by sight, and a dull lot they were. Whence came the men who made England great? pondered Mr. Milton. Certainly not from among his travelling companions, sheeplike to a man. The younger ones it was true essayed a certain distinction — or the reverse — in dress, but their behaviour appeared unexceptional.

One of the least remarkable of his unacknowledged companions was a small man, wooden of countenance, of taciturnity absolute. In the morning he gazed, invariably and apparently unseeing, from the window of the compartment. He read neither book nor newspaper, neither slept nor spoke. Thus had he travelled for many years. Therefore it was with intent, though concealed, interest that Mr. Milton one morning observed the man opening his brief-case. This may seem an unremarkable action, but it was so unexpected that it struck Mr. Milton as worth remarking. The event was however, immediately overshadowed by actions which would probably have surprised the most blasé commuter.

The man extracted from his brief-case a medium sized paper bag. Replacing his brief-case on the seat, he rose and turning to Mr. Milton enquired:

'Do you mind if I open the window?'

Mr. Milton, fascinated, silently shook

his head, whereupon the man knocked the bar catch, and slid down the window. The train was running through a shallow cutting, the banks of which were covered in scrub, low bushes, and tangled, blackened grass. Opening the paper bag, the man took out a handful of what looked like small striped beans. With a vigorous throw he launched the miniature projectiles away from the train, the slipstream catching them and whirling them away. Repetition rapidly exhausted the contents of the bag, after which the man folded it up and returned it to his brief-case.

During the following weeks, Mr. Milton kept a careful watch on his fellow passenger, but could detect no further signs of untoward behaviour. Nor did he offer any explanation.

Some months passed, and then in late spring, the man ceased to occupy Mr. Milton's compartment; ceased in fact to catch the train at all. A week after this sudden absenteeism, Mr. Milton caught sight of the man's photograph in a local paper. He had died of cancer after a prolonged struggle with the dread disease. The photograph headed a fulsome obituary which concentrated on the man's hobby of horticulture which had won him many prizes in local shows.

'So,' mused Mr. Milton, 'it seems I shall never know what he was up to.' In this, however, he was mistaken. As spring burgeoned into summer, he noticed an unusual type of vegetation appearing on the embankment at which the deceased traveller had hurled his missiles. Stalks, with large green leaves at intervals, thrust their way skywards, six or more feet off the ground, and presented large blind discs towards the trains. Then one day, one of the discs opened, and a flower peered forth. The next day it was fully open, a huge, bright yellow sunflower blazing against the drabness of tired scrub and worn-out grass. Soon the whole bank was ablaze with the fresh yellow of the sun.

Each succeeding spring, the fallen seeds of yesteryear's blooms germinated and the embankment brought forth its annual tribute to the dead commuter. A shame, thought Mr. Milton, that he didn't live to see the fruit of his sowing, but at least I shan't forget him.

'Remembrance was not the only consequence,' went on Hugo. 'I do believe it was that story which engaged my youthful mind with the oddities of human behaviour which in due course led me to the study of social anthropology. It is in the profusion of unintended results of the multifarious actions of multitudinous individuals that the richness of human life is generated.'

I demurred.

'Don't you think,' I said, 'that if it hadn't been that tale it would have been some other circumstance that would have directed you to your current interests.'

Hugo shrugged.

'Who can tell? I certainly don't believe in fate, still less predestination. I can easily imagine having pursued a different career. Was there no seminal event in your early life directing you to chemistry?'

I had no need to think deeply.

'Yes,' I admitted. 'I am convinced it was a first year chemistry lesson at the grammar school when we added ammonium hydroxide to copper sulphate solution. I was captivated by the beautiful blue crystals we used to make the solution and then by the instant change to a powder blue on addition of the hydroxide, drop after drop until the whole solution had changed, and then on as the precipitate redissolved to form the deep blue cuprammonium ion. I had never seen anything so fascinating! I believe my career was chosen at that moment.'

'I can believe it,' commented Hugo wryly. 'I don't think I have ever heard anyone describe a chemical experiment with such fervour!'

Artistic License

For a city so vast and thronged with people as London, it is astonishing how often one meets acquaintances quite by chance. Perhaps if these apparently fortuitous encounters ware analysed they would seem less remarkable. For instance, although I was surprised to bump into Hugo Lacklan in Piccadilly I suppose I ought not to have been. I was emerging from Burlington House where I had been consulting some volumes of a Russian journal of chemistry in the library of the Royal Society of Chemistry; and Hugo, I learned, had just come from the Museum of Mankind which lies directly behind it. Given our respective disciplines, his anthropology and mine chemistry, it might be considered almost inevitable that we should meet thus!

Hugo explained that he was acting as a consultant in the planning of an exhibition of ritual masks from New Guinea to be held in the museum, which is the

Ethnographic Department of the British Museum.

'The curator must be a brave man or a desperate one to enlist your aid!' I remarked. Lest this seem a churlish gambit I should mention that Hugo is the only Fellow ever to have been expelled from the Royal Anthropological Society — the Royal Ants as he calls them — and that was for a dignity destroying practical joke he perpetrated at one of their meetings. He'd been invited to give the Huxley Lecture, but that's another story.

'You're looking very brown,' I continued.

'I've just returned from a week on the Mediterranean littoral of Turkey,' he answered.

'Yet another holiday?'

He contrived to look pained.

'That's not the sort of remark which should sully the converse of one scientist with another. You can hardly regard an anthropological expedition as a vacation.'

I smiled.

'So it was science that took you to Turkey.'

'No, not really,' he admitted, 'at least not in the way you mean it. I went to try and help a friend. Look I might as well tell you all about it; I think it might interest you; it impinges upon your own field in a way.'

'All right,' I conceded, realising too late that I'd let myself in for another of Hugo's tall tales. 'But over coffee! Reading Russian papers is thirsty work.'

'Good idea. The Ritz?

I was scandalised.

'I wouldn't drink in that monument to vulgarity even if I'd just read the whole of Izvest Akad Nauk!'

Hugo chuckled.

'I believe there's an unpretentious coffee house in Dover Street. Let's try that.'

When we were comfortably settled with a pot of Blue Mountain coffee between us, Hugo returned to the object of his recent visit to Asia Minor.

'I was asked to go out there by an old friend, Jack Scowen. Do you know him?'

I shook my head.

'I thought you might as he's a chemist

himself. I hadn't heard from him for quite a while and then all of a sudden I received a long letter from him, written from a Turkish jail. He explained how he had ended up there and asked if there was anything I could do to help him. The story he told was certainly an intriguing one and although I wasn't too sanguine, as I could combine a trip to Turkey with work further to the north of the area he was in, I went out there feeling that personal contact might be more effective than an impersonal written plea.

'As I'd read Jack's letter I could almost hear the man himself speaking to me — he was from Bristol, you know, with a relaxed accent, admittedly somewhat at odds with the tale he had to tell.' Hugo proceeded to relate the contents of the letter, quite likely verbatim, knowing Hugo's phenomenal memory. He couldn't resist doing the accent as well, so that as I listened to his assumed Bristolian drawl, I too could easily imagine that it was Scowen himself speaking.

* * *

It all began the day I met Aubrey Hunt. I was a relative newcomer to the company's installation near Iskenderun at the eastern end of the Mediterranean. I'd been sent out from England to manage the chemical complex and I was still having trouble getting to know what was what and who was who. That morning had been particularly tiresome. I'd bumped into Ted Rowlands while I was out at his end of the site. He was supervising the laying of a pipeline down to the shore.

'What on earth is that for?' I demanded. 'I haven't authorised anything of this sort.'

'We need more cooling water,' he explained.

'But the complex already has an intake from the river,' I pointed out.

'I'm perfectly well aware of that,' replied Rowlands irritably — and a little impertinently I felt, 'but we need to test the effectiveness of cooling with water direct from the sea. It's part of the development work on the new pilot plant for D-273.'

'I still didn't authorise it,' I persisted.

'Sorry,' answered Ted grudgingly. 'Didn't

think you had to. I thought it was within my powers as Deputy with responsibility for development.'

'Well it isn't,' I snapped. 'Company regulations clearly state — oh let it go this time, but please do try and follow proper procedures.'

By the end of the afternoon I'd had more than enough of the day and almost didn't go to the expatriate party at Edgar Winthrop's. I didn't know anybody at the party, but our host was of the sink or swim school and didn't bother with introductions. I drifted about with a sweetish but pleasant enough tasting local beer in one hand, the other hand in my pocket drying itself on my handkerchief in case I had to shake hands with anyone. Phew! it was hot!

Most of the other guests seemed to he Scottish or Welsh, discussing 'Britain' in uncomplimentary terms as people who've made their homes abroad seem to feel compelled to do. Somehow being in a foreign country accentuated the tribal differences between myself and these Celts and Gaels, instead of bringing us closer together as Britons. So I was glad when I heard the somewhat affected tones of Aubrey Hunt. Back home I'd have avoided like the plague anyone who spoke like that but at least he would be English, or if from one of the other British tribes would nevertheless have been trained to rise above the tribalism!

In fact it transpired his home ground was the Cotswolds, and since I knew that part of the country well, we were able to carry on a reasonably convincing conversation. It came out that he was an artist, and then of course I remembered having heard his name in connection with something at the Royal Academy. Now he'd exiled himself to capture sunshine and sea on his canvas, as a change from the wide open skies and ochre earth of the wolds.

He manoeuvred us towards the doors which opened on to the balcony, and passing through we stood looking out over the bay.

'Isn't it magnificent?' he demanded. 'That one scene I could paint and paint and paint again, and never tire of painting it. The sweeping curve of the bay, the rising headlands — and the sea, so calm, so clear — and now and again the merest ripple to catch the fire of the sun. Look at the bare and ruddy earth, and the pitiless blue of the sky, and then the soft coolness of the water.'

It certainly was beautiful and I felt a sense of timelessness creep over me. We stood for some while there on the balcony until at length Aubrey Hunt stirred.

'You must come and see my pictures,' he commanded rather than invited. 'There are so few English folk of sensitivity here or anywhere if it comes to that. I don't think there are any at all in England.'

I felt somewhat flattered by this commendation, though realising well enough that what he took for sensitivity was merely a propensity I have for daydreaming whenever I'm exposed to sunshine. Nevertheless I accepted his invitation and some days later I stood in the artist's studio.

Aubrey Hunt's house was higher up the hillside than any I had yet visited and this produced a welcome coolness. The studio had high windows overlooking the bay. I crossed to them and stared out at a view similar to the one Aubrey and I had enjoyed before.

'Ah, my dear fellow,' remarked the artist, 'like me you can't get enough of it — the view I mean.' He chuckled.

'It is delightful,' I murmured.

Aubrey Hunt frowned momentarily.

'Not quite the word I would have chosen,' he reproved. He brightened again.

'No matter, come and look at these.'

He indicated a pile of canvases in a corner of the room. While I watched he placed them in turn on an easel, and then stood back for a suitable interval for me to admire them. They were all paintings of the bay and they were all remarkably similar.

'I paint it every day,' he remarked, as though having read my thoughts.

'But the bay doesn't look exactly the same every day,' I objected.

'What's that got to do with it?' asked Aubrey.

There was something else odd about the paintings. The sea was bright green! It was almost the colour of grass, yet the Mediterranean Sea beyond the window was indisputably, beautifully blue.

'Why have you chosen that particular shade for the sea?' I asked — quite forgetting that Aubrey Hunt was a celebrated artist, and I an artistic ignoramus. However, he showed no sign of being offended.

'Why have I painted it green, you mean?' I nodded.

'It's the way I see it,' he replied simply. 'Or perhaps you might say the way I wish we could all see it. Green is so much more restful than blue, especially in this sun-drenched country, where everything is parched, where there's no grass and even the green of the trees looks dry and brittle.'

'If you feel like that you should go back to England,' I said. 'There's plenty of wet grass and grey-green sea there.'

'But I like it here,' answered Aubrey, somewhat plaintively, 'all except for that outrageously blue sea. Can't you see how much better my green sea harmonises with the brown of the earth, and even with the blue of the sky. Besides an artist's mission in life is to improve on nature, not simply to record it.'

He certainly had a point. The intense blue of the sea could be rather tiring to the eyes and there was no relief in the sky or on the earth. We chatted on a bit, until I said I'd have to be getting back to the works.

'I wouldn't mind looking round the complex sometime,' said Aubrey.

'You'd be welcome,' I replied, 'although I wouldn't have thought it was really in your line.'

'Oh we artists find inspiration in the most unlikely places,' answered Aubrey airily.

As I took my leave it struck me how spacious and well furnished the artist's flat was.

'You must make a good living from your painting,' I commented.

'Hardly anything old boy,' he countered. 'Roy Matthews the financier pays for all this lot. He's my patron you know — very lavish.'

'He must be very keen on art.'

Aubrey sniggered. 'He knows next to nothing about art and cares even less. The last time I spoke to him I was talking about The National and he thought I meant the Grand National instead of the National Gallery. No, he's got his eye on the honours lists — patron of the arts; he's hoping for a life peerage. All I have to do is spread the word I'm his protégé — preferably in the ears of friendly civil servants.'

It was a week later that Aubrey Hunt came to look round the plant. I gave him the layman's tour and he peered vaguely at pipes and valves, and stared up at the reaction vessels with a disdainful air. We were making our way to the dining room — a wooden hut near the admin-block — when I was bleeped. I dashed into the nearest office and grabbed a phone. It was nothing serious but it needed immediate attention, so I left Ted Rowlands, as my deputy, to entertain Aubrey over lunch. Rowlands is an impecunious blighter, always eager for a meal at the company's expense. However, he seemed to have earned his lunch as when I got back Aubrey Hunt was in a very affable mood. I felt rather relieved. It had crossed my mind that if there was to be any local opposition to the further expansion of the plant, then Aubrey Hunt was just the sort of person to lead it — hence my anxiety to sweeten him. I went home feeling fairly pleased with myself.

The next day I found Rowlands down by the pipe again.

'You and Aubrey Hunt seemed to hit it off very well together.'

'Oh — yes, well we have interests in common,' he muttered.

'Really?' I raised my eyebrows. 'I didn't know you were an artist.'

'I dabble a bit,' replied Rowlands stiffly. 'Do you mind if I get on now? Sorry to be unsociable but I do want to get this pipe laid so that we can start trials.'

'Of course,' I agreed.

Disaster, when it came, came with devastating speed. I had moved into a more expensive flat, further up the hillside where I too had a view of the bay. I was woken early one morning by the telephone. It was the mayor of the nearby township. His normally broken English

189

seemed to have been completely fragmented and my Turkish although improving couldn't cope with speed or excitement, but at last I gathered there was something wrong with the bay, and he wanted me to go and look at it. I laid down the receiver, and rose reluctantly from my bed. The carpet was soft under my bare feet as I padded through into the living room, and across to the picture window which opened onto the balcony and its view out to sea.

The bay was a pale turquoise green.

I can hardly describe my reaction to the sight — a mixture of disbelief, of longing to awake from a nightmare, of rage, of self-pity, of self-criticism, and of apprehension. The day was a kaleidoscope of ugly incident. It soon became quite clear that Aubrey Hunt had grown so obsessed with the idea that his colour scheme was superior to the natural hues, that he'd bribed Rowlands (with Matthews' money — no life peerage for him after all!) to produce a dye using the pilot plant, not the red dye Rowlands was supposed to be investigating, but a deep sea green. Rowlands had used the cooling water pipe to discharge the dye into the sea. The outfall had been located close to the river which ran into the bay, and this had aided the dispersal of the dye.

We were all arrested and charged with conspiring to pollute coastal waters. Aubrey Hunt admitted his actions with pride rather than contrition. He had, in his own opinion, wrought a vast improvement over Nature. Rowlands had no real defence — he'd acted solely out of greed. He'd done as Aubrey wanted and been well paid for it. As for me, I pleaded total ignorance and was told I ought to have known what was going on. I was found guilty of negligence.

The dye is likely to persist for a very long time I'm told. Through the window of my prison cell you can see the bay. It is a very restful scene; the blue sky, brown earth and the green of the sea.

★　★　★

I was silent for a while when Hugo had finished, then asked:

'How long did he get?'

'Two years.'

'Two years in a foreign jail! What an appalling prospect.'

'Daunting enough anywhere — some of our own prisons aren't anything to be proud of — and there are worse places it could have happened. He hasn't committed a political crime and he isn't Greek, so they'll treat him tolerably. Even so it's a big slice of a life to lose, which is why Jack sent for me. He remembered that I have contacts in Istanbul and hoped I might be able to help him.'

'And could you?'

'As I said I wasn't very hopeful but I looked up a friend of long standing — a lawyer as it happened which was particularly useful — and told him the whole story. He saw the funny side of it and, more importantly, could see that Jack was more of a fool than a knave. He's promised to do what he can to have the sentence reviewed.'

'Do you think he'll succeed?'

'I'm hopeful. Part of the trouble was, of course, that Scowen's command of Turkish was woefully inadequate to cope with a situation of that sort. Muzaffer Bey is a wily old devil. He'll be able to present the admitted facts in an entirely different light. If he's lucky, Jack may escape with a deportation order. Still it all goes to show doesn't it, that artists are dangerous folk — almost as much of a hazard as chemists!'

Proof?

The train clattered across points and swayed. I smiled and nodded companionably to Hugo Lacklan who sat opposite me, his back to the direction of travel. We were both tired, having spent a strenuous day striding the Ridgeway path, a walk which we had been doing in sections, as opportunity arose. Today we had pushed on after we perhaps should have called a halt, knowing that we were almost at the end. Dusk was falling as we skirted Pendley Manor on the edge of Tring, and we ascended the incline beyond Tring Station through the deepening gloom of woods, lent enchantment by the uncertain light. By the time we had negotiated the last mile of the ridge and reached the summit of Ivinghoe Beacon it was truly dark. The northward sweep of the Vale lay below us, mysterious except where twinkling lights proclaimed tiny settlements. Above us the summer triangle of

Vega, Deneb and Altair to the south and the familiar saucepan shape of the Plough to the north twinkled as though in answer.

In silence we trudged the few miles back to Tring Station where we caught a Euston bound local train, looking back with satisfaction on a day in the open, and forward with anticipation to hot baths and a good meal.

It was as we left Watford Junction that there was a particularly violent jerk, followed by hard braking which brought the train to an abrupt halt. All the lights went out. A moment later the feeble glow of the emergency lighting system relieved the dark. It soon became clear that we were likely to be marooned for a while. Vandals had dropped copper wire onto the overhead cables and shorted the power supply.

Hugo sighed.

'It seems we shall have to exercise some degree of patience,' he remarked, 'if irritation is not to spoil an otherwise satisfying day.'

'Don't you have a suitable story to

regale me with, while we wait?' I asked mischievously.

'That depends on what you mean by suitable,' he countered. 'I do recall a somewhat unusual and ultimately tragic episode that had its inception on a train journey, but it has no other relevance to our present situation.' He reflected for a space while I waited patiently.

'It happened to a former student of mine,' he said at length, 'by the name of Alun Thomas. He wasn't in any way an outstanding student, but he was a pleasant enough chap, although rather introspective. The events I have to describe occurred some years after he'd graduated. No one, I think, knows exactly what happened, probably not even poor Alun really understood, but I will relate matters as I reconstructed them in retrospect.'

As always Hugo was quite unable to state the facts baldly but must elaborate them. I have not tried to sift fact from whatever might be Hugo's fancy, and what follows is, as nearly as I can remember the tale he told me in the

196

gloom of the stranded train although I in turn may have embroidered it. If so I assure you it is not intentionally but through fallible recall.

★   ★   ★

Alun Thomas didn't normally speak to people on the train. In fact if he saw anybody he knew on the platform he avoided them if he possibly could. He liked to spend the journey to and from work catching up on his reading, not wasting it in idle conversation. So he was not very pleased when the man in the seat opposite spoke to him, especially since the man was a complete stranger.

'I don't suppose you'll be very pleased at my interrupting your reading,' said the man. 'But I see we have an interest in common.' He indicated the book that Alun was reading, *Clairvoyance, Fact or Fable?*

'Indeed,' answered Alun, in his most discouraging voice.

'Yes,' replied the man. 'My name is Stephen Stanfor.'

This did interest Alun. Stephen Stanfor was somebody of whom he'd heard, or rather read. He'd seen Stanfor's advertisement in *ESP*, the magazine whose advent was the highlight of Alun's month. He recalled now, Stanfor was the man who offered to supply applicants with photographs of how they would look during each of the next twenty-five years.

'I've seen your advertisement,' admitted Alun.

'Indeed,' said Stanfor in turn, 'I had a feeling you might have. But you haven't responded to it,' he continued, with a grin.

'Two hundred and fifty pounds is quite a lot of money,' replied Alun, 'and I don't quite see the point of it anyway.'

'Don't you,' said Stanfor in surprise. 'But that book you're reading — why are you reading it?'

'Why?' asked Alun, puzzled.

'Indeed,' repeated Stanfor. 'To sum the book up, it's an attempt to persuade the sceptical that clairvoyance is fact, am I right?'

'Yes,' agreed Alun.

'So the fact that you're reading it seems to mean two things. Firstly, that you'd like to believe in clairvoyance, and secondly that you can't quite make up your mind to do so. Am I correct?'

'I hadn't thought of it quite so starkly as that,' said Alun, 'but, yes, I suppose that must be so.'

'Good,' continued Stanfor, 'then for two hundred and fifty pounds I can resolve your doubt, and in the most interesting way possible, a way which involves yourself as the central piece of evidence. I think it's a bargain at two hundred and fifty pounds. I admit I'd like to do it for you for nothing, simply as a scientific experiment, but I have to live and I'm not going to waste my time working in a factory, leaving my gift to wither away from disuse, when by charging a modest fee for exercising it, I can give all my time to my real work. So for two hundred and fifty pounds I guarantee to supply anybody with a set of twenty-five photographs showing them how they will look during each of the next twenty-five years. If for any reason I can't do that — for older people I often can't for obvious reasons — then I refund the money or an appropriate proportion.'

Stanfor paused. Alun said nothing.

'I find it easier to concentrate on one year at a time,' resumed Stanfor, 'and it's quite a drain on my faculties, so I usually select a group of people and provide them with a twenty-five week course. The first week I produce photographs of them all for next year, the following week for the year after next and so on.'

'How do you 'produce' these photographs?' asked Alun.

'It's quite simple in principle,' replied Stanfor. 'I have a roll of film with me during a session, and a photograph of each of the people participating. I throw my perception forward into the year I'm studying and then concentrate on the first photograph. Gradually a new picture forms in my mind — a picture of how the person will look at some time during the year in question. Often the change is not very marked, unless the person grows a beard, or has their head shaved, or some such thing. As soon as the picture is fully formed in my mind, I transfer it to the roll of film, simply by willing it there.'

Alun looked out of the window. He saw the train was nearing his own station.

'I get off at the next stop,' he said. 'I'm very pleased to have met you. I've found it very interesting.'

'Think about it,' urged Stanfor. 'I'd be very pleased if you'd participate. I feel it's important that people like yourself who are sympathetic should give themselves the chance to become convinced. Only when a large enough group of people are thoroughly convinced themselves can we hope for scientific recognition of the facts.'

The train lurched to a stop. Alun struggled with the door catch, and then was out on the platform. He waved to the face of Stanfor, blotched and distorted through the dirty windows. As Alun shuffled along in the pack of commuters funnelled towards the station exit, he fretted about Stanfor's proposal. Then he decided it was no use thinking about it until he was home and relaxed.

Alun lived by himself in the top flat of

an old five storey house. Most of the flats had huge chill chambers, but the top one was fashioned from the attic and servants quarters and had low, curiously shaped, but cosy rooms. Alun prepared his meal in the tiny kitchen, then sat down with a sigh in his armchair in the living room. He put a record on the turntable — Elgar's piano quintet. Chamber music suited the square low-ceilinged room, and suited too his own mood. He relaxed and ate. As he ate he leafed through the last month's copy of *ESP* until he found Stanfor's advert. He read it carefully, then putting the magazine aside he thought about the matter.

Why was he so reluctant? True, two hundred and fifty pounds was a good deal of money, but he probably spent that much in a year on books about extrasensory perception. He could afford it. Did he have some premonition of what the photographs might reveal? Was he in fact afraid? If so, then he should ignore his fear. Science was not a pursuit for the timorous, any more than for the parsimonious. Suppose the experiment were successful: he would know for sure that clairvoyance — and by implication extra-sensory perception in general — was no dream. Somehow that certainty was very important in his life. If Stanfor should fail, it would prove nothing, except that Stanfor was not always successful, and might even be a charlatan. So what it really came to was this; was he willing to risk two hundred and fifty pounds, and perhaps some unpleasant surprises, for the possible prize of certainty about extra-sensory perception? If he didn't take the chance he might as well admit to himself that he wasn't really serious about the paranormal.

Alun wrote to Stanfor that night. Stanfor replied saying how pleased he was that Alun was joining him in this important enterprise, and that he could expect the first photograph in a few weeks.

When it came, Alun was slightly dismayed. It looked like him, and yet it did not. He compared it with a duplicate of the recent photograph he had sent to Stanfor. Was the difference simply that to be expected in a man one year older?

He compared the current photograph with one he'd had taken perhaps two years ago. These two were at least as different as the current one and the future one. The more he looked at it, the more convinced he became that it was possible. The following week brought a second photograph, and now he could see the progression of slight changes which made up the imperceptible effect of ageing. The third and fourth photographs carried the process gradually further.

The fifth photograph was a sickening shock. The picture was still recognisably himself, but terribly altered. His cheeks were hollow his lips were thin and bloodless and his hair grey, his brow was lined and there was a look of fearful apprehension and pain about the sunken eyes. What dreadful suffering, mental or physical could have produced so abrupt a change? Alun's imagination supplied him with too many unpalatable possibilities. All the rest of that week he was haunted by the thought that some terrible experience awaited him, only four years away.

He found it impossible to discount the

prophecy of the photographs. He knew now that his belief in clairvoyance was firm and unshakeable. Had the photographs revealed a slow ageing to a distinguished looking middle age he would have remained sceptical. The terrifying impact of the fifth photograph was all too convincing.

Alun awaited the arrival of the sixth photograph with apprehension amounting almost to dread. He had no immediate family, and no friends close enough to confide in. The awful aspect of the fifth photograph continued to work on his nerves and cast him into a state of depression. At first he put the photograph away, determined to try to forget it, but he was unsuccessful. The hideousness of it grew in his mind, until he must look at it again to reassure himself that the actuality was not so terrible as he imagined. But the photograph itself seemed more terrifying than at first. He noticed new signs of suffering.

By the time the sixth envelope arrived, Alun could hardly bear to open it. There was no photograph! He sighed with relief, and sat down in a chair for a few minutes.

Then he took up the letter which was in the envelope in place of a photograph. As he did so, a cheque fell out. It was for two hundred pounds. The letter said:

'Dear Alun,

I very much regret to tell you that I was unable to obtain an impression of you six years from now, so I am returning the balance of your contribution.

I hope you will not feel this necessarily portends some personal disaster for you in five or six years from now. I cannot claim to be infallible after all, and there may be reasons I do not know of why I should be unable to obtain an impression.

I shall be interested to hear how your appearance matches the photographs you have already received, in the years to come; that is if you should care to write to me.

Yours sincerely,
Stephen Stanfor.

Alun was aghast. Despite Stanfor's disclaimer of infallibility Alun was convinced that in a few years time he would undergo some horrible experience that would lead to an early death. He could not shake off this conviction. He went to work and returned in a dream, a dream of nightmare quality. That evening he set an enamel plate on the kitchen draining board and made a small heap on it of the torn-up photographs and letters. He set fire to the pile, and when it had all burnt away, he pounded up the ash and washed it away down the sink. But he could not so easily destroy the canker in his mind. His first horrified reaction deepened into apprehensive fear, and then depression. He lost all interest in eating. He could not sleep. He performed only routine tasks at work and these listlessly. Finally it was suggested that he take a holiday and pull himself together. He sensed an implied 'or else' in the suggestion.

At this point, Alun had uttered a belated cry for help, in the form of a long, rambling letter to Hugo, from which he deduced the history he had related to me. He wrote a reply with some urgency, but it arrived too late to influence the course of events. It was because the letter had been found on Alun's doormat by the policeman who broke down the door that he was called to the inquest as a witness.

Alun Thomas' next of kin was a cousin, David Evans. David was surprised to be summoned to London to identify his cousin's body, even more so to learn that he had committed suicide.

'Of course I didn't know him well, you understand,' he told the coroner's enquiry, 'not recently that is. When he went away to London we sort of lost touch. Not a great boy for writing, wasn't Alun.'

'So you've no idea what may have driven him to take his own life?' asked the coroner.

'No I haven't,' agreed David. 'I can't say as I'd like to live in London myself, but he could always have come back to Wales if he was that fed up.'

'Hm' said the coroner. 'What do you know about his interest in — humph — psychical research?'

'Nothing at all except that he must have become interested in it after he came to London. There was nothing peculiar about Alun before he left Cardiff.'

'I have a letter here,' said the coroner, 'which was among those delivered to his flat the day after his death was discovered. The clerk will hand it to you. Will you please read it and see if you can cast any light on it.'

Evans took the letter and read it. Then he shook his head.

'Means nothing to me,' he said, 'never heard of the man.' He returned the letter to the clerk, who was asked by the coroner to read the letter aloud.

'Dear Alun,
   'I'm afraid I made a terrible mistake. Those photographs I sent you were not future likenesses of yourself, but of someone very similar to you, psychically as well as physically. The mistake arose because I can in fact gain no impression as to your appearance a year from now. As I said before, this does not necessarily mean that anything serious will have happened to you. It may simply be my fallibility.
   'I enclose a cheque for the difference

between *your fee and the amount already refunded.*

'*Yours sincerely,*
'*Stephen Stanfor.*'

'There's little more to add,' concluded Hugo. 'The inquest was adjourned while attempts were made to contact Stephen Stanfor, but these were unsuccessful. He had vanished, as do so many people every year. Perhaps more effort would have been made if there had been any indication that he had perpetrated some crime, but he had returned all the money he'd been sent, and there was really no doubt that Alun had committed suicide. Such was the coroner's eventual verdict, with the usual saving qualification of 'while of unsound mind'.'

'What was your own verdict?' I asked.

Uncharacteristically, Hugo hesitated.

'I couldn't decide,' he said at length. 'As scientists we both know that in individual cases we can't always be sure about causes. The general laws may be undoubted but which ones operate in a particular instance we can't always determine. Like lawyers

we have to settle for the balance of prob-
abilities. As well as the human tragedy of
Alun's death there is the philosophical
tragedy that it didn't prove anything.'

Hardly had Hugo finished speaking,
when the train lights came on and the
motors began repressurising the braking
system. I stared at the window. The
darkness had turned it into a mirror in
which I glimpsed my own face, subtly
distorted for a moment, as though it had
aged suddenly.

Allergy

All this took place some time ago but I have been reluctant to record it because it disconcerted me not a little and even now I will have to steel myself not to minimise its import. If I were to accept it without reservation, I would become a frightened man so I prefer to assure myself that Hugo is mistaken. However I am at last ready to let people judge for themselves.

Hugo Lacklan and I sat on the terrace of Cylcaster Hall, sipping coffee, and looking out across the rose gardens to the herbaceous borders and well-mown lawns beyond. He was on one of his frequent visits to London — his attention to the metropolis being such, indeed, as to cause some of his colleagues to suggest that he should perhaps be listed as a Professor in the University of London, rather than at his own institution in the north. Anyway here he was, and here I was, Hugo having rung me and suggested an outing to

Cylcaster. I was nothing loathe as I'd been feeling a bit under the weather, but the white chairs and tables gleaming in the sun, the aroma of coffee, and the air of languid civilisation were already having a beneficial effect.

As we relaxed in the sunshine I was teasing Hugo about the tall tale he'd spun me last time we'd met. He has something of a reputation for these stories, even mixing them into his undergraduate lectures on social anthropology. Any student unwitting enough to include one of his outrageous fictions in an examination answer being guaranteed a very poor mark, of course. To critics, Hugo offers the explanation that it teaches them to think for themselves; to sift fact from fantasy; and to accept nothing on one man's authority.

Anyway, he tried one of these stories on me the previous winter, and I must admit it had disturbed me a bit at the time, but I put much of that down to the gloomy atmosphere of the medieval fortress his college owns and where Hugo has his rooms. Sitting basking in the sunshine of Cylcaster I could laugh at it for the nonsense I was sure it must be, and forgive Hugo his persistence in maintaining it was all true.

It really was a beautiful day and the only fly in the ointment was the slight malaise my cold engendered. As if prompted by this thought, I sneezed violently three times.

Hugo raised his eyebrows.

'Hay fever?'

'No, no,' I answered, 'just a summer cold.'

'I hope you're right,' he responded, in such a grave tone that I was quite startled.

'Even if I weren't, hay fever's nothing to worry about. It's an inconvenience rather than a disability after all.'

'So Magnus Thoren used to say. You remember him?'

I nodded.

'I haven't seen or heard of him for ages. I wonder what happened to him?'

I ought to have known better than to offer so tempting an opening to Hugo. I could almost see his mind move into a higher gear as he drained the remains of his coffee, and settled more comfortably in his chair.

'As a matter of fact,' he remarked, 'I'm probably the only person in the world who can answer that question with any real certainty.'

I grinned ruefully. Hugo certainly had the knack of arousing one's interest.

'All right,' I conceded with mock resignation, 'I'm listening. Let me in on the secret.'

'Did you know him well?' he parried.

I shook my head.

'We were undergraduates together, and I came across his name from time to time in College newsletters and conference reports. Oh yes, and we once sat next to each other at a reunion dinner; but even as a student he was rather withdrawn; I don't think any of our contemporaries really knew him well.'

Hugo poured more coffee.

'I first met him when we were both assistant lecturers in Leeds,' he said. 'Although our academic interests didn't really coincide, we were in the same department and so became quite well acquainted. When I left Leeds, however, we lost touch. I heard he'd moved to London, the way one does, but I wasn't especially interested. Then, suddenly, out of the blue, he came to see me. He was up in Durham for a conference, and said he'd thought he'd look me up. It soon became apparent, however, that it wasn't just a social call. He was eaten up with anxiety about something, although at first he couldn't bring himself to spell it out.'

'I dare say it didn't take you long to fathom his secret,' I jibed.

Hugo grinned.

'I had to anaesthetize him first! I fed him the best part of a bottle of madeira. He didn't seem to appreciate the wine, but it did eventually have the desired effect.

'He was worried about his brother Erik. He didn't come out with it quite so bluntly as that of course and I'll approach the subject in the way he did, since it has a bearing on what comes later — unless of course you're finding this a bit of a bore.'

I assured him I was absorbed.

'Well then, Thoren had two consuming and related interests — his hobby was gardening and his work was in plant genetics. He waxed lyrical over the beauty of his garden in spring, when everything was new and fresh and he spent a lot of his spare time working in it. Summer was not so pleasant for him, since he suffered very severely from hayfever. Mowing the lawn was bad enough, he told me, but scything the long grass was awful and even sitting in the garden was likely to make him sneeze, his eyes itch and his nights wheezy.

'He was equally enthusiastic about his research. He found the microscopic structures of plant cells as beautiful as their macroscopic forms, the nomenclature of his subject — chloroplast, cytoplasm, protoplasm as lyrical as the names of the flowers he grew in his garden — stardust, love-in-the-mist, honeysuckle and heartsease.

'Strange,' he confided to me, 'that the objects of my interest and affection should cause me so much suffering in return. But then perhaps not so strange. The same is often true in human relationships.'

'Thoren was not married. His parents were dead. The only family he had was his brother, older than himself, but in many ways dependent on him — a drug addict, unable to keep a steady job, steady friends, or anything at all steady. His only link with the ordinary acceptable world was through Magnus. Magnus got him out of trouble, went bail for him, stood surety for him, put him up, put up with him, listened to him, gave him money, forbore to give him advice, in fact did everything that the relationship demanded. He expected, and got, nothing in return. As he put it, the beauty of his flowers gave him pleasure, despite the distress their pollen caused him. What pleasure did he derive from his brother's existence? 'None', he said, but he knew that was not exactly true. If he tried to imagine what life would be like if his brother no longer existed, he said he felt a degree of loneliness that he found difficult to understand. Erik was, perhaps, the only person who really needed him. Anybody else could do his job, teach his students, probably even do his research which he admitted was not startlingly original. Everything he did was for his own personal satisfaction — his work, his pleasures, music, gardening, painting — everything that is except being a brother.'

I was astonished that Magnus Thoren should have confided so much to Hugo, for after all they were comparatively distant acquaintances, and Thoren was such a reserved fellow. I saw that Hugo Lacklan was observing me quizzically.

'You find this baring of the soul difficult to believe?' he remarked drily. 'It didn't all come out quite so lucidly as my account of it. A good deal I had to guess at, and the — ah — confessional occupied several evenings and depleted my cellar by some half a dozen bottles. Nevertheless I got the feeling that he had sought me out especially to unburden himself, as someone whom he knew but with whom he was not in frequent contact. On the last evening he asked me what he should do about Erik. I did what I could by giving him the names of some clinics where his brother could be quietly unhooked. My guess, though, is that it wasn't really advice he was seeking. He just wanted someone to whom he could speak in confidence.'

I was beginning to feel uneasy about Hugo's revelations. Even if he were just spinning a yarn, the central character was real enough and I was puzzled by Hugo's uncharacteristic lack of discretion. Flamboyant though he was, he had a sensitivity for the feelings of all but the pompous.

'Are you sure you ought to be telling me all this?' I ventured. 'I mean I'm not one to gossip, but the more people who share a confidence the more likely it is that one of them will let something slip.' Hugo was not to be diverted, however. He made a dismissive gesture.

'It must have been a decade before I saw Thoren again,' he went on, 'and then it was quite by chance. I got on a train at the Bank and there he was, sneezing his head off. It was midsummer, and even underground it was almost intolerably hot. Magnus always had suffered from hay fever, and when I commiserated with him he seemed eager to talk about some ideas he had on the subject. Although I was going only to Bond Street, there had been some sort of accident and we were stuck in that wretched train for a considerable period, quite long enough for him to tell me a remarkable story.

'It seemed that one summer, several years before, had been particularly uncomfortable for him. There had been weeks of hot dry weather, when the pollen count reached record levels. As he travelled to work in the crowded trains, be had been confronted by the evidence of other people's sufferings — sneezes, red eyes, irritability. An old man who spoke to him on the underground said he'd never had hay fever in his life until that year, but now he had 'the snuffles'. It must, he groused, be the high pollen count.

'Thoren mused on the old man's grumbles. Did everybody have a threshold level, above which they would suffer an allergic response? That didn't seem reasonable, since the experimental studies on hay fever all pointed to specific allergies. People were either allergic to something — pollen, spores, cats, whatever it was — or they were not. But Thoren began to wonder how much of that was assumption — and how much proven fact. He felt it was something that might be worth looking into sometime.

'During the long vacation when Magnus would normally have immersed himself in his research, taking advantage of his students absence, he had found himself balked by the non-delivery of a vital piece of apparatus. At a loose end, he had finally persuaded himself that it was a good opportunity to catch up on his reading and had made his way to the library. He had selected a pile of periodicals and retired to a comfortable chair in a secluded nook. He'd found it difficult to concentrate on the 'heavier' journals. It was warm in the library and his laboured breathing had kept him awake the night before, so he turned to a popular scientific magazine and began to browse through the news and gossip columns. There were several snippets about hay fever, and a longer article tracing the history of research into allergies. From this piece it appeared to Thoren that really very little was known. What was needed it seemed to him, was sound statistical evidence about how many people suffered from hay fever, what sort of people they were, where they lived, how old they were, whether or not they'd always had it, or had developed it and when, and a hundred other points. Were men more prone to it than women? Negroes less than Caucasians? Indians more than Chinese? Old than young? Dwellers in town than country? He could think of dozens of questions to which there was at present no authoritative answer.

'So as a result of a series of minor events, Thoren began to take a serious interest in the problem. To obtain the information which might answer some of the questions that occurred to him, would be a mammoth task, but its potential utility far outweighed any of the research he'd done previously. He might even get financial. backing from the Medical Research Council!'

Hugo interrupted himself to reiterate

that not all of this had been spelt out by Thoren himself, some of it being inference Hugo had drawn. He drank more coffee before resuming.

'Thoren had returned to his office and begun drafting a questionnaire for distribution to doctors and their patients. He submitted an application for a grant from the Medical Research Council and also approached one of the big pharmaceutical firms for information on clinical trials into hypersensitization. As he worked at the problem his investigation gathered momentum. He was surprised at the amount of support he obtained. As the data accumulated, however, he became less surprised because it was obvious that the problem affected, to a greater or lesser degree, a large proportion of his fellow men.

'The enquiry had taken up more and more of Thoren's time. He had abandoned his experiments on plant cells. He interested postgraduate students in his hay fever survey and soon had a sizable group working on it. Results began to flow and papers to appear. The survey became world-wide and many people collaborated in it.

'The papers which Thoren published, on the incidence of hay fever among various races, ages and types of people were all strictly factual. I remember seeing some in journals in my own speciality, and they were models of their kind. But a suspicion was growing in Thoren's mind, as the years went by, that he was not studying a static phenomenon. The proportion of hay fever sufferers seemed to be increasing at a significant rate. At first he thought it was simply that his records were becoming more complete. Then he decided it must be that people were more aware of allergies than previously. Finally he came to believe that the increase was real. But he did not publish this conviction. The data on which it was based could be analysed in too many different ways.

'His belief did, however, lead him back to the laboratory. If hay fever was increasing, what was the reason? Were more people becoming allergic to the old allergens or were new allergens appearing.

'Thoren's studies had thrown up a

great deal of information on the sources of allergens, but very little on their real nature. This he began to study in detail, using his background as a plant cytologist as a starting point. Having a worthwhile goal, in the form of a question he passionately wanted to answer, revivified his capacity for original research and he attracted some outstanding students. Thoren's reputation grew. He was appointed to a chair. He was a success.

Hugo paused.

'Shall we stroll down to the lake?' he suggested and I readily agreed. He went on almost immediately.

'At the time of our meeting on the underground, Thoren was really at the peak of his career. Again we lost touch for a while but I couldn't help noticing that his publication rate began to fall thereafter and one heard odd comments about some of his theories being unsound.'

I smiled at this. It was an adjective frequently applied to Hugo's own ideas.

'I must admit I was surprised to receive, out of the blue, an invitation to attend the funeral of Erik Thoren, Magnus' brother, who had finally died from his addiction. I travelled down to Oxford by train and was met by Magnus at the station. It seemed the family came from Great Neblington, a small village some ten miles outside the city, and there was to be a service at the Oxford crematorium. Magnus and I and an ancient aunt were the only mourners. The aunt left immediately after the ceremony and Magnus and I went back to the family home. Although he worked in London, Thoren had kept the house on and often spent weekends there.

'Thoren showed me into the library, his favourite room. Three walls were covered with book-lined shelves, broken only by a door leading from the passage. The fourth side was all glass, and looked out onto the garden. A paved terrace led to a broad lawn edged with flower borders, backed with shrubs and trees. It was twilight. The trees stood black against the darkening sky. The scents of eventide wafted through the open windows. The garden was peaceful but for Thoren there was a certain menace lurking behind the surface calm. He loved his garden, knew and loved each plant individually. His hay fever was an affliction, no fault of theirs. But a dark suspicion had begun to grow in his mind, and as we sat in the gathering dusk he confided his fears to me.

'It's common knowledge that people sometimes die from allergic responses; from the accidental injection of foreign protein or from the sting of a bee. About two years before, a report had come to Thoren of a man dying during a severe attack of hay fever. He was a middle-aged man, and the doctor had certified heart failure, perhaps aggravated by the hay fever attack. Magnus had written to the doctor and despite the latter's reluctance to divulge case details, Thoren had been able to satisfy himself that there was no history of heart disease and nothing to account for the seizure. Several similar cases had since come to his notice. It began to look to him as though hay fever was turning into a killer. Were people becoming more sensitive to allergens, he asked himself again, or were there suddenly more violent allergens about? He decided that the second possibility was more easily tested.

'He collected pollen samples by filtering air through paper discs. From the discs he extracted the pollen and separated it from the soot and dust also trapped. The pollen extract he tested for allergen reaction and compared his results with ones he had obtained years before, by noting the reaction of rats to a subcutaneous injection of the extract. He was horrified by the result. Instead of the null response or small red weal which he had previously observed, four of the animals died and the fifth became seriously ill.

'With the help of his students, Thoren repeated and extended the tests, with the same depressing results. Convinced that there was a new and deadly allergen abroad, Magnus began a thorough investigation of the trapped pollens to try and identify the virulent agent. Isolation of the allergen was an arduous task, but eventually he had it in pure form. It was a protein. Analysis of its structure showed that it included a number of amino acids not previously found in nature. This fact staggered Thoren. He could not understand how the presence of the amino acids had gone undetected until now.

'He was able to identify the pollen grains that he had trapped, from their microscopic structure. The pollens of about half a dozen different grasses were present. He instructed his students to collect samples of the grasses and these he tested for the presence of the new amino acids. The tests were positive and unmistakeable.

'On a hunch, Thoren tested some samples of the same grasses collected ten years previously. Tests for the amino acids were negative. Thoren hesitated to draw the conclusion that the amino acids and the proteins constructed from them were new plant products, but he could see no alternative.

'He tested a wide range of plant samples and whenever possible compared them with older samples. The pattern persisted. A large number of plants were synthesising new amino acids and from them constructing new proteins producing marked allergic responses in rats. Thoren tried a minimal skin test of one of the new proteins on his own arm. It gave him a three-day fever, swollen eyes, racking asthma — and left a red weal on the site of vaccination.

'The following summer was bad for Thoren. His hay fever became almost unbearable. Millions of other people experienced a similar worsening of allergy symptoms. Thoren estimated that several hundred people actually died from hay fever, although nobody else recognised the true cause of death. Hay fever seemed to have spread to areas of the world where it had never before been experienced. Even high mountain areas and the open sea were no longer free of it.'

'Really Hugo,' I interrupted, 'I'm disappointed in you. This is most implausible. If what you — or Thoren, if you insist — as I say if these claims were true they'd've been all over the scientific press — even the national press.'

Hugo stopped and swung round to face me.

'You think so?' he enquired mildly, a mildness belied by the elevation of his eyebrows! 'You are wrong, you know. The learned journals were already set against Magnus and his theories. He'd stopped sending papers to them, for they simply rebounded with the addition of a rejection notice. And the national papers? Well, yes one of the tabloids might have run the story in the silly season, but that would hardly give it credence! And as for the more sober dailies and Sundays they wouldn't risk being made fun of. No, even if Thoren had tried to publish, no one of any consequence would have given him space. Oh, they'll wake up to it eventually, then you'll see some headlines! But by then it may be too late.'

'Too late?' I cried. 'Whatever do you mean?' But Hugo was silent. I tried to adopt a reasoning tone. 'But someone else would have noticed the things Thoren did, would have reached the same conclusions,' I objected.

Hugo was impatient.

'You're naive,' he answered. 'There are very, very few people with really open minds. Most, scientists included, run in very narrow grooves and haven't the courage to poke their heads out of them.

Still, if you aren't interested either . . . '

I was stung into agreeing to hear him out, and he resumed as though my interjection had never been.

'Sitting alone in his home one evening, Thoren reviewed the situation. He decided there were two salient facts — firstly, more and more people were suffering from hay fever and it was a new and more violently allergic form; secondly this novel type of allergy resulted from new proteins being synthesised by plants and incorporated in pollens. In addition there was a suggestive but incomplete indication — he had been unable to distinguish any useful function of the new proteins. Its only property seemed to be to increase allergic response by animals to the pollen. The obvious, although astounding conclusion to draw was that plants were deliberately increasing the allergic effect of their pollens. There was no conclusive evidence that this was so, but it was consistent with what he knew. It appeared to Thoren that plants — flowering plants at any rate — had at last devised a means of hitting back at their persecutors in the animal kingdom.

'The more he thought about it, the less outrageous it seemed. Plants had always sought to protect themselves against animal predators by producing and storing poisons in vulnerable parts. He reflected how extraordinarily successful the stinging nettle had been in defending itself. Hay fever had always been regarded as an unpleasant by-product of pollination. But perhaps it had all along been an evolutionary experiment by the flowering plant community to find a more effective weapon against animals. If so, the weapon would seem to have reached a new and deadly stage of development.'

We had reached a small summer house and I was grateful for the shade it afforded. The sun was hot and the heat seemed to bring out my cold. My eyes were slightly puffed due I supposed to my having spent too much of my time in front of a VDU. Hugo and I sat down on a bench where we had a fine view of the lake and of the water-loving plants around it.

'I never saw Thoren alive again,' resumed Hugo suddenly.

I was startled.

'I didn't know he'd died,' I said.

'He had rather faded from the scientific scene,' Hugo reminded me. 'His theories weren't welcomed by the editors of learned journals and after their initial amusement at his eccentricities, fellow biologists began to be rather irritated by them. I suppose they felt he made them all look faintly ridiculous.'

I sneezed violently. Damn the cold and damn viruses, I muttered to myself. Hugo regarded me with an expression of genuine concern.

'I really do hope that is no more than a cold.'

'You don't mean you give any credence to Thoren's wilder ideas do you?'

'I was present at his inquest,' responded Hugo obliquely. 'The aunt had died by then; he'd no friends, and he'd isolated himself from his colleagues. There were some letters from me among his effects and on the strength of these the coroner summoned me and asked me about his state of mind.'

'He didn't commit suicide did he?'

'The coroner decided not but there

was something of a mystery about his death. The doctors put coronary on the certificate but I spoke to one of them and he admitted in a guarded way that he was puzzled. The postmortem produced no evidence of deterioration, yet he certainly seemed to have succumbed to a massive seizure.'

Hugo was silent for a while. It was a depressing tale and I wasn't quite sure why Hugo had recounted it. Usually there was some moral to his stories, or at any rate a question posed.

'Anyway,' I returned to my earlier point, 'you haven't told me whether or not you thought there was anything in his theories.'

'Oh I do,' he answered unexpectedly, 'most certainly I do. As I said at the beginning I think I know how he met his death, although I'm not so sanguine as to expect anyone else to believe me.

'Imagine, if you will, Magnus Thoren seated in his library at Great Neblington. It's late. He sighs, stretches and stands up. He walks over to the window and looks out. It is dark but he's been sitting without the light on and his eyes are adjusted to the gloom. Besides there's a full moon and the garden looks cool, mysterious and inviting. He slides open the glass doors and steps out onto the terrace. The air is refreshing. He moves slowly down the steps and across the lawn towards the shrubbery. Among the taller plants it is darker. The stems and leaves brush against him almost affectionately. The branches make intricate and pleasing patterns against the night sky.

'He broods on the theories he's been working on. His garden is the source of so much pleasure to him. Can he really believe that the plants in it could become as inimical to him — and to all animal life — as his researches suggest? It seems impossible.

'He turns a corner, knowing the garden so well he could have found his way without the aid of the moon. He comes to the heathers. First those of winter, now just a mass of foliage, but then the summer ones in full bloom, the white flowers ghostly in the moonlight. He stops. How absurd to see danger in such beauty. He draws a deep breath of the cool night air . . . and chokes. He takes another breath, struggling for air, wheezing and coughing. His eyes begin to stream and between the coughs he tries to sneeze. His skin is tingling. He attempts to draw breath again and cannot. Slowly he sinks to his knees on the path, gasping and retching, then falls forward, his lifeless head cushioned by the summer heathers.'

In the silence that followed I stared, horrified, at Hugo Lacklan. At length I made an attempt to break the spell his words had cast over me.

'Preposterous,' I protested weakly. 'There's no reason to imagine any such thing, no evidence at all.'

Hugo sighed, and then smiled suddenly.

'I dare say you're right. I do have a fertile imagination after all. Yes, I suppose there must be some perfectly ordinary explanation for his death. Even if I am right, it may be that his experiments had hypersensitized him to allergens or perhaps his belief in his theories prompted a psychosomatic seizure. It would be over-reacting to assert that his death proved he was right.'

A bout of sneezing made me feel quite wretched and we left Cylcaster Hall soon afterwards. I was glad Hugo had to return north that night. He wasn't the convivial company he usually was; or perhaps my cold had made me depressed.

A Nineteenth Century Dream

'Some time ago my grandfather died and in due course his personal effects and papers were passed to me as his only living descendant. Among these papers were some journals which had belonged to my grandfather's uncle, Joseph Macbaine. Uncle Joseph was a medical practitioner in the early nineteenth century and he rather unprofessionally recorded details of his patients in his private journals. He didn't mention any names and it's too long ago for the people to be identified now, I should think, but at the time if the journals had become public, they might have caused a considerable stir in his remote practice. As it was, they gave me some amusement and caused me to reflect that life hasn't changed much since then — it's just reported more fully in the newspapers!

'There was, however, one quite singular case that I'm not sure how to evaluate. If you're in no hurry to get away, I'll tell you about it.'

We were sitting in Hugo Lacklan's room, just he and I. It is a curious room. The northern University where Hugo is a professor in social anthropology leases an ancient castle at a nominal rent, but it is nevertheless an enormous drain on the University's resources because of the cost of its upkeep. The original rooms of the castle were large and had been subdivided to reduce them to a more modern size. Thus Hugo shared half a window in the three-foot thick wall with the room next door. Plumbing and lighting sprawled across the stone like petrified creepers. He was however, fortunate enough to have a fireplace complete and we two were ensconced in huge armchairs before a blazing fire. We had not bothered to switch the lights on and so vast was the room that we seemed to be encamped beside a stone wall set in a barren plain.

The howling of the night wind was disturbing even through three feet of medieval stone wall and the fire was necessary as much for reassurance as warmth. Having settled myself in and warmed the chair, I was in no hurry to move. A good meal and wine had soothed my usual restless inclination to be doing and I was content to sit and listen to Hugo's rather precise speech. So I nodded and held out my glass to be refilled. Hugo resumed.

'An intelligent and cultivated gentleman — one of the few in Uncle Joseph's sparsely populated practice — had sought Uncle Joseph's advice about insomnia. Uncle Joseph was currently interested in the ability of Indian mystics to control their bodily functions and had collected as much information about the subject as he could. He would not of course have considered going to India, even if he had been in a position to, so his information was necessarily second-hand. Some of his ideas as described in his journal would have struck a guru as decidedly bizarre. Nonetheless he decided to see if this eastern knowledge could be of use in overcoming his patient's insomnia. The patient seems not to have been overenthusiastic about the idea — it was after all hardly suitable that an English gentleman of the early nineteenth century should indulge in native rituals. Being nearly at the end of his tether however — and nineteenth century Englishmen were bred with extraordinarily long tethers,' (I smiled dutifully and somewhat sleepily) 'he agreed to have a go.'

Hugo paused and refilled his own glass. Doubtless even Hugo became dry when talking, 'though he'd never been known to dry up completely.

'Uncle Joseph taught the man the necessary exercises. They worked. By the time the man had mastered the Eastern arts as interpreted by Uncle Joseph, he was sleeping like a top. He was not in fact a great deal happier however.'

I was beginning to get interested.

'The trouble was that his sleep was visited by dreams of merciless clarity and extraordinary persistence after waking. The dreams did not seem to be connected in any sequential fashion, but they did make a consistent whole. Uncle Joseph recorded these dreams exactly as the man had related them or so he claims and I've no reason to disbelieve him, but I'll condense some of his descriptions by using our words for the things he is so obviously describing with difficulty.'

Hugo stirred the fire and sparks flew up the wide chimney. An owl hooted and I settled deeper into my chair.

'In the first of these dreams it was night. The man was walking along a beach, white in the moonlight. To his left heaved a black sea; to his right the land was low and bleak. Clouds passed occasionally across the moon, and then he had to stop for fear of stumbling in the dark. The sand gave way to shingle and curved away to his right. Soon the shingle in turn yielded to large stones and occasional rocks. He scrambled up on to the higher ground, which was covered with springy turf. A cloud was over the moon. His eyes strained towards the south trying to see something.

'Then the cloud fled from the moon's face and the scene was bathed in silvery light. The low promontory on which he

stood ran down to a headland only a few
feet above sea level. A stone jetty, low
but broad, ran out from the end of the
peninsula into the sea. Waves broke across
it. But all this was of only secondary
importance, a dark surround for the
central feature. On a square quay, higher
than the jetty, were two large spheres,
silver-grey in the moonlight. They seemed
to monopolise the moon's light, like twin
moons themselves, resting on the quay. In
an instant the dreamer was beside them,
looking up at the nearest globe which
curved up and away from him. Now he
could see it was artificial, made of
cunningly joined metal plates. To one side
of the two spheres was a square, squat
building. He noticed light streaming
from a window, then he was inside the
building.

'There were three men in the block-
house. One was seated at a console before
an array of dials, switches and lights.
Another stood before a similar display.
The third was making notes in a ledger.
Through the window the dreamer could
discern the outline of the globes, seen

dimly from the brightly-lit interior. The three men seemed unaware of him, but talked among themselves. The language was English, but many of the words were unknown to him. 'Power' was repeated many times and he thought he heard the word 'station', but there was no sign of trains or tracks out here on the edge of the wild sea.'

Hugo paused.

'The dreamer woke but the vision left him uneasy, and prompted by Uncle Joseph's interest, he related the dream to him. It was the first of a number.'

Hugo busied himself for a few minutes, putting coal on the fire, refilling our glasses and then resettling himself in his armchair.

'In the second dream, the dreamer seemed to be in a wide, very long low room. There were no windows but the room was well lighted artificially. A chasm ran the length of the chamber and disappeared into a tunnel at each end. The tunnels were pitch black with no sign of daylight. On approaching the channel he saw it was only a few feet deep and

that rails ran along the bottom. The scene then seemed to him to be more familiar than that in the previous dream. He felt, indeed, that he really was in some kind of station, though one unlike any he had heretofore seen. His impression was confirmed when a train of four silver coaches emerged from the tunnel at one end of the room. It came very fast and there was no smoke. It was all lit up inside and full of people. At this point he noticed that there were others besides himself on the platform. The train stopped, doors opened, passengers flooded out. There was a brief melee round the doors, before people from the platform surged into the already crowded carriages. The doors flowed together and the train accelerated from the station at a frightening rate, its tail lights finally winking out in the gloom of the tunnel.

'The dreamer observed several more such trains, before himself feeling impelled to enter one. He fought against the compulsion but as so often in dreams, he was powerless. He found himself crushed into a carriage, surrounded by other people who seemed not to notice him. The doors

closed and he was pushed against them. There was a thrumming and then the train surged out of the station and was surrounded by blackness. It bored on through the dark for what seemed an interminable period. The feeling of claustrophobia which the close confines induced in the dreamer, increased until it became intolerable. Suddenly the doors flew open and the dreamer was precipitated screaming into the dark — whereupon he woke up and slept no more that night.'

Hugo paused again. I had by now realised the point of the story — at least I thought I had. One can never be quite sure with Hugo whether he's telling something straight or spinning a yarn. One of his attractions as far as students were concerned, was his ability to present social anthropology in parables that were entertaining as well as pointed. I began to suspect that Hugo was simply trying out a spiel on me. Still, it seemed a good tale, the fire was warm and one bottle still unopened, so I merely moved in my chair to indicate I was still awake and waited for Hugo to continue. With some

perspicuity he first opened the final bottle of Madeira and refilled our glasses.

'The third dream was quite different from the other two but the dreamer claimed the sense of continuity was strong. He was standing at the bottom of a flight of steps made of a material resembling stone. The walls of the stairway were of a similar material and covered in graffitti. There was a strong smell of stale cooking with an undertone of something even less pleasant.

'The dreamer began to climb the stairs. It was cold and a chill draught pushed him forward. When he reached the first landing he found a narrow passage lined with doors. At the end was a grimy window. He looked out. It was night and the street below was lit by hard yellow lighting which revealed a few scraps of paper blowing in the wind, unemptied dustbins and the broken and dirty windows of the block opposite. The dreamer turned from this squalid scene to the door on his left. He found he could see through it. Inside were two rooms. In one of them a dozen people were huddled together, men, women and children, presumably for warmth. On a table were piled haphazardly a few cracked and greasy plates and some cups with the dregs of tea in the bottom. The faces of the adults were lined and apathetic, those of the children pinched but cheeky. The room was lit by a flickering bluish light emanating from an oblong box in one corner. The faces of those present were all fastened on this source of light and the dreamer found his gaze drawn irresistably towards it.

'He saw that the front of the box was of glass. On it was portrayed a picture, a picture that moved. Then he noticed the noise which seemed also to come from the box — the sound of people talking and of insidious, lulling music. The people on the screen were well-dressed in smart, if flamboyant clothes. The faces of the people on the screen were animated, laughing and talking, unlike those in the room, although the dreamer thought he perceived a certain blankness about the eyes of the people on the screen. They moved, stood or sat in a room luxuriously furnished. They had food to eat, wine to drink. Their faces betrayed no cares. The contrast between the scene portrayed on the screen and that evident in the room was stark.

'The dreamer passed to the next floor. The same poverty oppressed. So he rose to the ninth floor, where in a freezing attic an old woman lay completely immobile beneath a pile of blankets. It was with relief that the dreamer passed through the roof of the building, up and away into the clear starlit sky. Below him more stars appeared to twinkle — the lights of a vast city, here and there cut by the snaking ribbon of a well-lit road.

'So ended the third dream. In the fourth the dreamer was on a street in what seemed to be a large town. The street was deserted. At one end vehicles, concrete and wreckage barred the roadway. All down the street, shop windows were smashed and glass littered the pavements. He heard a noise and turned. A strange, windowless vehicle had entered the thoroughfare from the other end. It saw the barricade and seemed to hesitate, then moved forwards. An avalanche of sound greeted it, cracks and explosions. A cannon mounted on the vehicle replied and part of the barricade was shattered. More vehicles were coming including one with an immense shovel in front. A detonation close by showered more glass and rubble into the street. Still the dreamer saw nobody; it was as though this battle was being fought between the inanimate and the unseen. A stunning explosion brought the dream to an end and the dreamer woke.'

Hugo paused and I took the opportunity to interpose a comment.

'This is all very ingenious,' I said, 'as a way of highlighting the absurdities of modern civilisation — describing facets of it as seen through the eyes of a man of the last century; but I wouldn't overdo it, if I were you.'

'You are wrong,' protested Hugo. 'This isn't one of my devices for imparting social anthropology painlessly.' He rose and moved away into the gloomy outer reaches of the room. When he returned he had a leather bound volume in one hand

and another bottle in the other. He leafed through the book until he found a page he was looking for. He handed the book to me, saying simply:

'Uncle Joseph's journal.'

I studied the faded writing and the worn binding. It all looked genuine — a very elaborate fraud if it was a fraud and to what purpose? I read a few sentences. It was almost word for word the account of the fourth dream as just related by Hugo.

'All right,' I said, 'I'm half convinced. Clairvoyance is a possibility admitted by many people after all. This patient of your great-great uncle may indeed have dreamed of what life could be like in the 20th or even the 21st century.'

'Clairvoyance's literal meaning is clear seeing, not necessarily of the future and indeed it was originally limited to the faculty of seeing at a distance,' replied Hugo pedantically, 'but given that the details of the patient's dreams would not have existed in the nineteenth century, they must either have arisen from seeing the future or from a vivid imagination. I

hope for our sake it is the latter, for I have
yet to recount the final dream — or
perhaps you'd rather read what Uncle
Joseph himself wrote?'

I turned a few pages and found an
entry headed *The Fifth Dream*. The hand-
writing was good and I began to read.

*I had a further consultation with the
former insomniac, wrote Uncle Joseph.
He has had another dream. I can do no
better than report his description of it
verbatim:*

*I found myself once again in the
surroundings of the first dream. The
moonlight glinted on the leaden sea. A
cold wind found its way through my
clothes and chilled the marrow of
my bones. Snowflakes whirled past me
and were swallowed up in the molten
ice of the sea. I stumbled along the
beach, impelled by the freezing wind
towards the headland. As before, I
scrambled up a bank and then I could
again see the jetty with its two spheres,
silver in the moonlight. The thought
came to me that it would be warm and*

dry in the block-house, that there
would be shelter from the knife-sharp
wind. I picked my way carefully down
to the jetty and then set off towards the
quay. Dry, powdery snow was collecting on the jetty, the wind stirring it and
piling it in little heaps against the stone
parapet that ran along the west side. In
the moonlight, the snow-covered surface was pale turquoise. I reached the
quay and clambered up the steps. The
silver globes were as before; no snow
settled on them. I turned to the
block-house. It was in darkness. I
hurried to the thick window which
looked towards the spheres. It was
smashed. Round the back I found the
door ajar and pushing it open I stepped
inside. All was ruin. Dust, broken glass
and rubbish mingled to form a detritus
of dereliction. All was abandoned.
Through the gaping window I could
see the perfect spheres — did they still
perform their function? Or were they
also lifeless? I could not tell. The
presence of disaster I felt oppressing
me. So I woke.'

I stared at the page awhile. My head had cleared and I felt cold inside. I closed the volume and handed it back to Hugo. He read my thoughts from my face. Together we stared, in silence, into the dying embers of the fire.

THE END